"Can I count on you to help me?"

"Yes, sir." Charlie nodded vigorously up and down then slanted a glance at Meg before turning back to Cole. "You can count on both of us."

"Is that right, Meg?" Cole lifted a sardonic brow. "Can I count on you…this time?"

The words stung as much as if he'd slapped her. Yet, for Charlie's sake, she managed to keep a smile on her lips.

The nerve of the man. He acted as if it was *she* who'd let him down all those years ago rather than the other way around.

Snapping the last piece of equipment into place, Meg scrambled to her feet and held out a hand to him. She met his gaze. "Of course you can trust me, Cole. Every bit as much as I can trust you."

Dear Reader,

When my daughter was small, I worried what would happen to her if her father and I both died before she was grown. Luckily we had some wonderful relatives who agreed to step in and raise her if that happened. I had no doubt they would love her as their own.

In *Jackson Hole Valentine,* Charlie's parents are killed in a car accident. But in their will, instead of specifying a couple to take and raise their child, they name two single friends! On the surface that decision makes no sense. As Margaret says, it's as if they handed over custody of their precious son to a divorced couple!

Thankfully, in this book set in beautiful Jackson Hole, not only do Meg and Cole get their happy ending (thanks to being brought back together by the provisions in the will) but little Charlie gets his, as well.

I don't know about you, but I wouldn't have it any other way.

Happy reading!

Cindy Kirk

JACKSON HOLE
VALENTINE

BY
CINDY KIRK

First published in Great Britain 2013
by Mills & Boon, an imprint of Harlequin (UK) Limited,
Eton House, 18-24 Paradise Road, Richmond, Surrey TW9 1SR

© Cynthia Rutledge 2012

ISBN: 978 0 263 90090 3
ebook ISBN: 978 1 472 00450 5

23-0213

Cindy Kirk has loved to read for as long as she can remember. In first grade she received an award for reading one hundred books. Growing up, summers were her favorite time of year. Nothing beat going to the library, then coming home and curling up in front of the window air conditioner with a good book. Often the novels she read would spur ideas, and she'd make up her own story (always with a happy ending). When she'd go to bed at night, instead of counting sheep, she'd make up more stories in her head. Since selling her first story to Mills & Boon in 1999, Cindy has been forced to juggle her love of reading with her passion for creating stories of her own…but she doesn't mind. Writing for Mills & Boon® Cherish™ is a dream come true. She only hopes you have as much fun reading her books as she has writing them!

Cindy invites you to visit her website at www.cindykirk. com.

To my fabulous critique partner and friend,
author Renee Ryan. This one's for you!

Chapter One

Margaret Fisher glanced around the attorney's waiting room, her heart fluttering like a hummingbird on steroids. Too nervous to concentrate on the magazine in her lap, she took a couple of deep breaths and let her gaze linger on her surroundings.

The random-width plank floor made from exotic woods added visual appeal while the muted tan-colored walls provided the perfect foil for the "artwork" in the room. Like many businesses in Jackson Hole, the designer had carried the cowboy theme a bit too far for her liking. Ryan Harcourt's rodeo awards were featured prominently on the wall and a well-oiled saddle sat on display in one corner.

Despite Ryan having graduated from a prestigious east coast law school, there was not a diploma in sight. Margaret assumed there would be one in his office. It didn't surprise her to see him focus on his roots in the outer waiting area. In Jackson Hole, the majority of his clients would relate better to his rodeo background than to his Ivy League education.

The young attorney—and former champion bull rider—was well-known to Margaret. He'd been a classmate of hers at Jackson Hole High School as well as a close friend of Margaret's boyfriend, Cole Lassiter. Not boyfriend, she corrected herself. Cole was simply the jerk who acted as if he loved her, took her virginity and then unceremoniously dumped her, all without taking her on a single date.

It had been years since she'd seen Cole. She'd half expected their paths to cross at the funeral. After all, growing up, he and Joy had been next-door neighbors. Margaret had also heard he stopped in to see Joy and Ty whenever he was in town. But then, Cole hadn't bothered to come to her parents' funeral so it hadn't surprised her when he didn't show. *Respect* didn't seem to be a word in his vocabulary.

"Charlie, would you like to play with these?" Lexi Delacourt, the social worker seated to Margaret's right, opened the large colorful bag and let the child she'd brought with her peer inside.

Margaret smiled as the boy's eyes brightened, and she pushed aside the old memories. There were more important things to think about today. Cole was the past. Today was about her future. Just like it had been when she'd sat in the attorney's office on her seventeenth birthday. That day she'd been with her seven siblings. The normal laughter and joking that always occurred when they were all in the same room had been noticeably absent.

It was understandable, of course. They'd been stressed and grieving. Anxious about what was going to happen to them now that their parents had died. She wondered if Charlie had that same sick feeling in the pit of his stomach she'd had back then.

She cast a sideways glance at the little boy who was now

lining up plastic dinosaurs on the rough-hewn top of the wooden trunk coffee table. The six-year-old was the son of Margaret's childhood friend, Joy, and her husband, Ty.

Now they were both gone, killed in an accident only weeks before Christmas near Brown's Curve on Route 22. The same stretch of Jackson Hole roadway where her folks had died.

It's not fair.

Tears stung the back of Margaret's eyes. Though she hadn't seen as much of her friend as she'd have liked since leaving Wyoming fifteen years ago, thanks to the internet and cell phones, she and Joy had remained close confidantes and friends.

Without warning, Charlie jumped up from the brown-and-white cowhide sofa, his boots making a loud thud on the floor.

"I'm gonna look at the fish," he announced to Lexi when she cast him a questioning look.

He crossed the room looking adorable in his blue chambray shirt, jeans and cowboy boots. He'd been wearing something similar in the picture Joy had emailed Margaret last summer, the one taken at the Lil' Buckeroo Rodeo in Pinedale.

Charlie had been a much-loved child. Her friend had embraced motherhood and Ty had doted on his son. Both wanted more children, but for some reason Joy had been unable to get pregnant again. They'd been trying since Charlie turned two and this past year had started expensive fertility treatments.

Margaret could understand why her friends had wanted more children. She'd fallen under Charlie's sweet spell when she'd returned to Jackson Hole last Christmas for the christening of her brother's twin babies. She'd been thrilled for Travis and at the same time envious of the way his life had so happily fallen into place. Before leaving town she'd stopped and spent time with Joy and her family.

When it came time for her to leave, Charlie had wrapped his arms around her and given her a kiss. Looping an arm around his waist, Margaret had teased Joy that she was taking him with her. But, as always, she'd left Wyoming alone, single seat on the aisle.

"They're ginormous." Charlie whirled around, his eyes wide with awe.

"Super big," Margaret agreed then sighed when he turned back to the aquarium. She'd once hoped to have a husband to love and a child just like Charlie to cherish. But she was already in her early thirties and that dream was looking less likely with each passing year.

As a physical therapist who dealt primarily with stroke patients, Margaret didn't have much opportunity to meet eligible men at work. And she'd never been one for the bar scene. To complicate matters, most of her friends were married. Of course, she reminded herself, if she'd been willing to exchange vows with a man she liked and respected but wasn't madly in love with, she'd be married, too.

But last year, after much soul-searching, she broke it off with her fiancé. She hadn't regretted her decision. Okay, maybe a couple of times on dark, lonely nights when she remembered how good he'd been to her and feared she'd simply been expecting too much. After all, they'd gotten along well and had fun when they were together. Did "madly in love" *really* have to be part of the equation?

She'd wondered.

Then she'd run into him and his new girlfriend a couple of weeks ago. The way they looked at each other told her she'd been right to call off the wedding. Not only for her sake but for his. Everyone deserved to be loved with such passion.

"Me an' my dad used to go fishing," Charlie said, gazing at the tank. "Mommy would sometimes come, too. But Daddy had to put the worm on the hook for her."

"That was nice of him." Lexi said. "You had a nice daddy."

Having Lexi overseeing Charlie's case felt almost like having a family member involved. When the attractive social worker with the sleek brown bob had introduced herself, she'd mentioned she was a good friend of Margaret's older brother, Travis, a local ob-gyn.

Margaret knew Travis and his wife, Mary Karen, had a group of close-knit friends. Like Lexi, all were married with children. Margaret sighed. Sometimes it felt as if everyone had the life she wanted…except her.

"Have you seen the will?" Lexi asked in a low tone, leaning over the arm of her chair.

Margaret shook her head. "But I have a good idea what's in it."

At the funeral, when Ryan asked her to come to his office for the reading, she hadn't been surprised by the request. Last year, when one of their high school classmates had died of cancer, Joy had broached the subject of Margaret raising Charlie if anything should happen to her and Ty. She'd been flattered but wondered why Joy wouldn't want her child raised by family.

Joy had informed her she'd already approached her parents. Apparently they'd stammered and offered a whole litany of excuses—they'd retired to Florida because of Larry's health, the gated community they'd just settled into didn't allow children, it would be best for Charlie to remain in familiar surroundings….

Margaret's heart had ached for her friend. All these

years Joy had been right. She'd always insisted that her
parents really had only one child—her brother—and that
she wasn't that important to them.

Ty's own family situation wasn't much better. He'd been
estranged from them for years. They'd sent a small plant
for the memorial service.

"Charlie, honey, don't press so hard against the glass,"
Lexi called out to the boy but made no move to get up.

With an older child and a busy toddler at home, this
was probably the only chance the social worker had to
rest. Margaret stifled a smile and rose to her feet. She
crossed the room, her heels clicking loudly on the hardwood. Normally she favored more comfortable clothing
than the silver-blue suit and certainly more sensible foot-
wear than high heels. But this had seemed an appropriate
day to forgo comfort for something more stylish and businesslike.

She crouched down beside the boy, who had his nose
pressed against the aquarium glass. "Which one do you
like best?"

"The yellow one." Charlie pointed to a large silver an-
gelfish with a blanket of gold over the head and back.

"It's very pretty." Margaret resisted the urge to brush
the tousle of chocolate-brown hair back from his face. "Do
you remember me, Charlie? I'm Margaret. I was a friend
of your mom."

The boy turned to face her, his eyes a deep, dark blue.
"Pastor says my mommy and daddy are with Jesus in
heaven."

Margaret took a deep breath and blinked back tears. The
sermon at the funeral had been comforting, but it was still
hard to accept that it had been her childhood friend lying
in one of the two caskets at the front of the church. Heart-

breaking to realize she and Joy would never laugh over the phone or Tweet pithy one-liners to each other.

Still, she believed the pastor when he'd said Joy and Ty were in a better place. Her friend had such a quirky sense of humor that Margaret had no doubt that at this very moment she was livening up the heavenly throng with Ty cheering her on.

"Do you think they're coming back for me?" he asked in a small voice.

"I'm afraid not," Margaret said softly. She cursed her honesty when his eyes filled with tears and his bottom lip began to tremble. "But I know they're still watching over you. And that they love you very much."

"I want my mommy." The boy's arms stiffened at his sides and his hands clenched into tiny fists. "Bring her here. Now."

Her heart rose to her throat. *If only I could bring her back. And Ty, too.*

Like a whirlwind sweeping across the plains, as quickly as Charlie's anger flared, it disappeared and he began to cry.

Margaret wrapped her arms around him, murmuring soothing words and holding him tight. After several heartbeats he quit struggling. After several more she felt him relax in her arms.

From her own experience, she knew a little about what he'd be going through in the weeks and months ahead. She vowed to make this transition as easy as possible for him.

With his soft curls still pressed against her cheek, Margaret heard the attorney's office door open. But she couldn't move a muscle. The child had his arms around her, holding her as tight as a drowning sailor would grasp a life preserver.

"Margaret." Ryan moved to her side and placed a hand

on her shoulder. "Lexi will take good care of him while we talk."

"Charlie, I have something really cool to show you." The social worker peeled the boy from Margaret's arms. "The office down the hall has some gigantic fish."

"Bigger than those?" Charlie pointed to the aquarium, his tears like little crystals on his long lashes.

"Oh, my goodness, yes. Way bigger." Lexi held out her hand. "Come with me and we'll go see them."

The little boy hesitated, glancing at Margaret.

"I'm not going anywhere," Margaret assured him. "I'll be here when you get back."

After a long moment, Charlie put his fingers in the social worker's hand. "I wanna see the fishes."

Lexi smiled at Margaret and gave the attorney a wink. "We won't be long."

Margaret watched them leave. Her heart warmed when Charlie returned her wave.

"I'm glad you could make it." Ryan gestured toward his office then stepped aside to let her pass. "We're waiting for one more but there's some preliminary stuff we can get started on."

Margaret smiled, finding it strangely refreshing to hear an attorney use the word *stuff*. She took a seat in front of his desk, wondering who it was Ryan was expecting. It hadn't crossed her mind that anyone else would show up for the reading. "Did Joy's parents change their minds and decide to stay in town a little while longer?"

"Nothing like that." The attorney took a seat in the cowhide-and-leather swivel desk chair and offered her an easy smile.

Despite being thrown to the ground and stomped on by bulls weighing close to two thousand pounds, Ryan looked no worse for wear. His face was unscarred and his hair as dark and thick as it had been in school. He was a cute guy but Ryan had never made her heart skip a beat.

Back then, people who didn't know him well had always confused him with Cole. Both had dark hair and slender, athletic builds. But Ryan's eyes were a silvery-gray while Cole's eyes were as blue as the ocean.

In her young, stupid days, Margaret had been convinced she could drown in Cole's eyes. She resisted the urge to gag.

Ryan shifted in his seat and glanced at his watch. Tiny lines furrowed his brow.

If Margaret didn't know better, she'd say he was worried. But that didn't make sense. What did he have to be concerned about? Unless he thought she was having second thoughts about raising Charlie. Could he be afraid she was going to bail on the boy?

Margaret leaned forward and rested both hands on the edge of the desk. "Joy and I talked last year about her and Ty's wishes, should anything happen to them. I'm fully aware that she wanted me to—"

The outer office door jingled.

Ryan's head jerked toward the sound.

Margaret paused and sat back.

Before she could say another word, Ryan leaped from his seat and rounded the desk. "I'll get it."

But he didn't have time to reach the door before it swung open. Turning in her seat to gawk at the new arrival seemed a little gauche, so Margaret waited for the visitor to stroll into view.

"It's good to see you," Ryan said.

"I hope I didn't keep you waiting long."

Margaret froze. The man's voice sounded all too familiar. She shivered as the sexy voice continued. "DFW got snowed in and all the flights backed up."

She didn't need to turn in her chair to know who Ryan had so warmly welcomed. Even after all these years, she recognized his voice. It was the same sexy rumble that had whispered sweet nothings in her ear when she'd been sixteen. The same husky voice that had shook with emotion when he'd pronounced her his sweetheart and given her a silver heart-shaped locket for Valentine's Day. The same voice that she hadn't heard again after they'd made love in the backseat of his old Chevy.

She dug her nails into her palms.

"You're lucky you didn't make it in yesterday morning. We had a jet go off the runway," Ryan rattled on. "Typical November weather."

"Anyone who grew up in this region should know better than to fly in the day of any event, especially at this time of year." Margaret turned in her seat, unable to sit still a moment longer. "Unless it was your intent all along to miss the funeral."

She had only a second to brace herself before Cole fixed his brilliant blue eyes on her, and to be startled at the sight of him on crutches.

"You remember Margaret Fisher." Ryan gestured to her with a broad sweep of a hand. "She went to high school with us."

It didn't surprise Margaret that Ryan would feel the need to clarify. After all, it wasn't as if they'd run in the same social circle back then. Ryan and Cole had been popular, while she'd been studious, shy and completely forgettable. A part of her had wondered if he'd ever mentioned his involvement with her to his friends. Apparently not.

Cole's expression gave nothing away. "Of course, I remember Meg."

"Meg?" Ryan lifted a brow. "I don't know that I've ever heard anyone call her that before."

That's because no one else ever had, only Cole.

"I meant, Margaret," Cole returned easily.

Ryan's eyes held a curious gleam and Margaret got the feeling he knew there was more to the story than a simple verbal faux pas.

"You're looking well," Cole said to her when the silence lengthened.

Other than the crutches and the brace on his right knee, she supposed she could say the same about him. His hair was a little longer now, brushing his collar in a stylish cut. The hand-tailored dark suit he wore emphasized broad shoulders and lean hips. Surprisingly, he'd foregone a tie and left his gray shirt unbuttoned at the neck.

While she grudgingly admitted that he looked…attractive…she had no use for him or for the words that came so easy to his tongue. Margaret lifted her chin. "Your friend appears to be too much of a gentleman to tell you—but this is a private business meeting."

She could have cheered when her tone came out cool with just the slightest amount of indifference.

Cole's brows pulled together and he shot Ryan a puzzled glance. "You told me this was the time you'd set aside to go over Ty and Joy's will."

Margaret narrowed her gaze and focused on Cole. "You must really be doing badly if you came all this way just to see if they left you anything."

For a second she regretted speaking so frankly. Being brash wasn't her style. Then she recalled how Cole had treated her and she decided she was being too kind.

"I'm doing quite well, not that it's any of your concern." Cole's expression darkened. He turned to Ryan. "What the hell is going on here?"

A look of guilt crossed the attorney's face and the gaze he shot her was filled with apology.

Margaret had always been intuitive. The unique gift that had failed her only once before was now telling her that something was about to go wrong. Dreadfully wrong.

"Ryan?" Margaret choked out the attorney's name, finding breathing suddenly difficult.

"Neither of you have the complete picture, not yet." Ryan gestured for Cole to take a seat then exhaled a harsh breath. "That's the way Ty and Joy wanted it."

Then this wasn't a chance meeting, but something orchestrated from the grave by Margaret's oldest and dearest friend. *Oh, Joy, what have you done?*

"I think I'd better sit down." With lips pressed tightly together, Cole moved carefully across the slippery wood floor and eased himself into the only empty chair in the room, the one next to hers.

Though a big part of her life revolved around physical rehabilitation, she didn't comment on his unsteady gait or ask about his injury. Quite simply she didn't care. She couldn't care. Not about him. Or his gimpy leg.

The only thing she wanted to know was why he was at this meeting…and how soon he'd be leaving.

Chapter Two

"I'm sure you're wondering why you're both here today." Ryan leaned forward across the desktop, his gaze shifting from Cole to Meg.

Cole decided the comment must have been directed toward Meg, because *he* knew exactly why he was here. Over Labor Day, Ty and Joy had told him they were finally getting around to making a will. When Joy said she'd love him to raise Charlie if anything happened to them, something in her eyes had confirmed his long-held suspicions.

Of course, he'd said yes. He'd been a part of Charlie's life since the boy was born. The only way Cole would let anyone else raise the child was over his dead body.

He glanced at Meg. Her eyes were focused on Ryan, her head held high. Just like the girl he remembered, she projected an air of supreme confidence. She'd always had high expectations of herself…and others. When she discovered he didn't measure up, she'd turned on him.

Cole clenched his teeth. The funny thing was, right now that memory hurt more than his leg.

The attorney steepled his fingers beneath his chin. If he noticed the tension in the room, it didn't show. "I'm not sure you know this, but Joy and Ty came to my office last month and made some changes to their will."

The comment didn't concern Cole other than he felt happy they'd followed through on what they'd discussed with him. He wished Ryan would get to the point, so he could pick up Charlie and get out of here. While he'd been prepared to see Meg at the funeral, running into her today had thrown him.

Damn Ryan for not giving him a heads-up. Then Cole realized the attorney couldn't have known it would be an issue for him to see her again. The only people who knew he and Meg had once been involved were Joy and Cole's brother, Cade.

When he'd first seen Meg his breath had caught in his throat. She was even more beautiful than she'd been in high school. Despite knowing he was playing with fire, Cole couldn't resist slanting another glance in her direction.

The beauty, which had showed such promise at sixteen, had been fulfilled. The red in her hair had deepened to a rich auburn, the vibrant color a perfect foil for her creamy complexion. From what he could see, her curves were still there, only more womanly than girlish. Her legs were as he remembered: long, slender and sexy as hell.

Ryan cleared his throat and Cole realized he'd been staring like a lovesick seventeen-year-old. Which he wasn't. Not seventeen. Certainly not lovesick.

"What k-kind of changes did they make?" Margaret asked.

Cole heard the uncertainty in her tone. Obviously Joy or Ty had promised her something. Though he couldn't imagine there would be much of anything left. The infertility treatments they'd been undergoing had taken all of their savings and then some.

Cole shifted position, hoping to take some pressure off his knee. The surgeon had warned him that if he flew so soon after surgery he was asking for trouble. Dr. Jones had been right. Even the extra leg room in first class hadn't helped.

He thought of the bottle of pain pills in his luggage with a twinge of regret but then realized even if they were in his pocket right now, he wouldn't take them. A man had to be alert to care for an active six-year-old.

"The change affects the custody of Charlie." Ryan cast an apologetic look in his direction.

In *his* direction.

Cole went hot, then cold. He told himself Joy wouldn't have cut him out of Charlie's life. And Ty, he'd talked about wanting his son to have a male role model if anything should happen to him.

None of this was making any sense. Not Joy and Ty making changes to their will that would cause Ryan to look at him apologetically. Not Meg being here. And certainly not the feeling which suddenly gripped him and whispered his life was about to be turned upside down.

"What kind of change?" Meg asked, her tone as tightly strung as a guitar string.

"This was a difficult decision for them," Ryan said. "Not made lightly."

"Quit talking around it, Ryan." Cole pinned his friend with his gaze. "Give it to me straight."

A look of gratitude filled Meg's eyes for the briefest of seconds before her lids lowered.

Cole scowled. He didn't want her gratitude. Didn't want anything except her gone.

Ryan stared down at the paper on the desk then looked up. "You're not going to like this—"

"Ryan," Cole growled, his patience depleted.

"Instead of giving sole custody to either one of you—" Ryan spoke quickly "—Joy and Ty decided that it would be best if you shared custody."

Meg gasped.

Cole swore he could hear her heart pounding. Or was that his? Regardless, he must have misunderstood. He cleared his throat. "If *who* shared custody?"

Ryan met his gaze. "You and Margaret."

"That's absurd." Meg's green eyes flashed, showing a bit of the spirit he remembered.

"Ryan." Cole gripped the sides of his chair until his knuckles turned white. "There is no me and Margaret."

"Their will is very specific on that matter." The attorney rose to his feet and smiled. "Now that we've got that out of the way, can I get either one of you a soda or a bottle of water before we go through the specifics?"

Margaret fought the urge to laugh hysterically. Her entire world had been turned upside down and Ryan wanted to give her a *bottle of water?*

"Forget the water," she muttered. "Give me a scotch."

She wasn't sure where the words came from. When she drank—which was rarely—she preferred wine over hard liquor.

Cole's hand dropped to massage his leg. "Make mine a double."

Ryan's eyes widened before he chuckled and reached inside a small refrigerator. "Three bottles of water coming right up."

Share custody with Cole? Was that really what the attorney had said?

Margaret closed her eyes. She had to be dreaming. Other than a nightmare, there could be no other explanation. But when she opened her eyes, Ryan was pushing a cold plastic bottle into her hand and Cole Lassiter still sat beside her.

"Read it again, Ry." Cole unscrewed the cap on his bottle. "Ty and Joy asked me if *I'd* raise Charlie if anything should happen to them. That was Labor Day weekend. Not even three months ago. They didn't mention one word about sharing custody with her."

Cole jerked a thumb in her direction.

"Well, when they asked me, they never said you'd be in the picture," Margaret retorted, even as her heart sank. If Cole was telling the truth, his conversation with Joy had been much more recent than hers.

"Children, stop right now. I want us all to take a deep breath." By the smile tugging at his lips, Ryan appeared more amused than troubled by their reactions. "There are some terms and conditions to being appointed Charlie's guardians. Terms you will need to carefully consider."

Margaret didn't need to consider anything. The little boy who'd sobbed in her arms needed her. Not to mention she'd promised Joy and Ty she'd take care of him. And, unlike the man sitting beside her, her word meant something.

Ryan took a sip of his water then gestured for her to do the same.

Although Margaret wasn't particularly thirsty, she brought the bottle to her lips and let the cool liquid run down her throat. To her surprise, she felt herself relax. This would be okay. Joy had been her friend. She wouldn't have put Margaret in a bad position.

Cole placed his water on the desk, a look of steely determination in his eyes. "I want to hear the terms, then I want a copy of the will for my attorneys to go over."

"Oh, *my attorneys*," Margaret said in a mocking tone.

"If that was an attempt to impress me—or perhaps even scare me—let me tell you right now, it didn't work."

His gaze met hers and for a second she recalled what it felt like to drown in those eyes.

"I run a business so I have attorneys." Cole's expression darkened. "Trust me, I couldn't care less if I impress you or not."

Trust him? Margaret would sooner trust a weasel. But trust him or not, if Cole had an attorney, she'd best get one, too. But while she knew several lawyers in Nebraska, they didn't deal with custody issues. Hadn't Lexi said her husband, Nick, was a family-law attorney? "I'd like a copy also. For *my attorney* to review."

Cole pressed his lips together and shifted positions.

"I'll get the papers run off for you," Ryan said, suddenly all business. "Now about the terms..."

Margaret reached into her bag and retrieved a small notepad and pen. As Ryan read, she took notes. Her horror grew with each additional stipulation. By the time the attorney finished, Margaret was ready to forget the glass of scotch. She needed a whole bottle.

"Let me get this straight." Margaret spoke slowly and distinctly in an attempt to calm her nerves. "We *have* to remain in Jackson Hole until the end of the school year?"

Ryan nodded. "Ty and Joy didn't want Charlie to face any more changes than necessary, at least not initially."

"But my job and my apartment are in Omaha." While Margaret had eventually hoped to one day move back to Jackson Hole, the reality was her life was in Nebraska. She could look for another position in Jackson Hole, but she still had four months left on her lease. No way could she incur the expense of moving and pay double rent.

"My company headquarters are based out of Austin, but I'll relocate to Jackson Hole immediately." Though Cole spoke to Ryan, he slanted a glance in Margaret's direction. "No problem."

Margaret could feel Charlie slipping away and for a second she felt powerless. Then she remembered something her dad used to say—*can't* was a word people used when they were unwilling to make sacrifices. Well, that wasn't her. She straightened in her seat. "I'll make it work."

A look of surprise skittered across Cole's face so quickly she wondered if she'd only imagined it. Nah, he was surprised. He apparently thought she'd roll over and play dead. Well, he'd soon realize that she wasn't that same shy sixteen-year-old whose heart he'd walked over and discarded like yesterday's trash.

"What happens after the school year ends?" Margaret asked.

"You're free to relocate back to Nebraska or Texas." Ryan took another sip of water. "But you'll continue to share custody. You'd have to make arrangements that will work for you and Charlie."

"I don't understand why they did this." Cole's mouth twisted. "Putting Charlie in the middle of a tug-of-war between the two of us couldn't be what they wanted for him."

Margaret was glad he'd brought it up. She'd been thinking the same thing. It was as if Joy and Ty had handed custody of their precious son to a divorced couple.

"They knew you both well enough to know you wouldn't let that happen," Ryan said, his expression suddenly serious. "They believed you would always put Charlie's welfare and happiness first."

Margaret stared down at her hands, praying she'd prove worthy of her friend's faith in her.

"That said," Ryan continued, "if either of you leaves Jackson Hole for more than a week at a time during this initial period, the other will be granted sole custody of Charlie."

Seven days wasn't a lot of time to quit her job, pack up her apartment and find a place to live in Jackson Hole. It was the last part that would be the hardest. In the ten years she'd been looking to come back, rent in the area had soared. And most landlords were demanding two months of rent as a deposit.

Margaret had money in savings but it wouldn't last long, especially if she had to pay an attorney. Once her money ran out, there would be no one to help. The only sibling with any disposable income was her older brother, Travis. Still, with five young children and a new house in the mountains, he had his own responsibilities.

"If you're not going to be able to do it," Cole said in a low tone, "it'd be best to back out now."

"That little boy needs a mother." Margaret met his gaze, her voice strong and sincere. "I'm not going to let him down."

Shortly after the copies had been made and another appointment scheduled for later in the week, the three made their way to the outer office.

Ryan was showing Cole his saddle when the door opened.

"Uncle Cole." Charlie's eyes lit up and before anyone could stop him, the little boy barreled across the room and slammed into him.

Cole felt the knee give way at the same moment Meg's arm slipped around him, giving him much-needed stability and a good strong jolt of déjà vu.

The light floral scent of her perfume, the feel of her body next to his…took him back to a time when she was his whole world. His body prickled with awareness.

Meg smiled down at the boy, seemingly unaffected. "Whoa, partner. Your uncle Cole just had knee surgery. Go gentle on him."

"I didn't mean to hurt him." Charlie turned to Cole. "Did I hurt you?"

Cole's heart melted and he shook his head.

A tiny frown worried Meg's brow. He could tell she found Charlie's exuberant greeting disturbing. Obviously she hadn't realized how close Charlie was to him. His smile widened.

"Honey," Lexi prompted, stepping forward and resting a hand on Charlie's shoulder. "Didn't you have some pictures you wanted to share?"

"I have one for you and one for you." Charlie pointed to Cole then to Meg.

"Hey, what about me?" Ryan asked in a teasing tone.

"Nope." Charlie's head shook back and forth. "None for you."

Ryan chuckled. "The story of my life."

Everyone laughed and Charlie looked up at Lexi. "Where are my pictures?"

"Right here, buckaroo." Lexi opened a large drawing pad and pulled out about ten different sheets of paper, with an assortment of pictures done in crayon.

Charlie slowly perused each one, his brows pulled together in thought.

"Thanks for catching me," Cole said in a low tone meant for Meg's ears only. Just because he wanted nothing to do with her didn't mean he couldn't be civil.

"If you'd gone down, you'd have taken Charlie with you," she responded in a matter-of-fact tone. "Couldn't have that."

Cole searched her cool green eyes. Though her expression gave nothing away, he had the distinct feeling she was angry with him. Which made absolutely no sense. If either of them had a reason to be bitter over their breakup all those years ago, it was him.

"This one is for you." Charlie shoved a picture into Cole's hand.

He glanced at the paper. Two stick figures, one big, one little, were standing by a bright blue lake under a huge yellow sun, fishing.

"I know this place." Cole smiled. "It's the lake where we spent the day together last summer."

"Yep." The little boy rocked back on his boot heels in a gesture reminiscent of Ty. "That's you and me."

Cole tightened his grip on the picture; the first Charlie had ever given him. It meant a lot to know the excursion had been a special memory, not only for him, but for Charlie, as well.

"Thanks, buddy." Cole tousled the child's dark hair. "I'll put this up in my hotel room."

"If you have a 'frigerator, you could put it there," the boy said with an eagerness that touched Cole's heart. "That's where my mommy puts all my pictures."

Cole exchanged a glance with Meg. Or maybe it was a wordless plea. It was getting close to the time Charlie had to leave and he wanted the encounter to end on as upbeat a note as possible. In a second he could see Charlie realizing that his mommy would no longer be putting up his pictures.

Meg seemed to understand, because she stepped forward.

"And what do you have for me?" She crouched down so she was at eye level with the boy.

"This one." Charlie brandished another picture with a flourish. "I 'membered you like flowers."

That much hadn't changed, Cole thought. When they'd

been together, Meg had loved all kinds of flowers. He wondered if daisies were still her favorite.

"You've got a great memory. And you're right. I do love flowers." Meg opened her arms to the boy. "Let me give you a 'thank you' hug."

Charlie went easily into Meg's arms, nestling his head against her shoulder.

Cole's heart gave a ping. He'd been feeling pretty good about the boy's greeting. And the picture, well, fishing was just the kind of thing a boy did with a dad.

But what he was witnessing now brought back memories of how his mother had been before his dad died and she'd turned man-crazy. She used to brush his hair back from his face and kiss his forehead, like Meg was doing to Charlie now. Would Charlie miss having a mother?

Cole shoved the thought aside. Certainly it would be ideal if he were married so Charlie could have both a mother and a father, but being single didn't mean he couldn't be a good parent to the boy.

"Do I get to go home with you and Uncle Cole?" Charlie slipped from Meg's arms and his gaze shifted from her to Cole. "My pajamas and Mickey Mouse toothbrush are in the car."

Ryan shot the social worker a questioning look.

Lexi smiled apologetically. "I wasn't sure how things would work today, so I packed his bag."

"It'll be a few days before we have all the arrangements made," Ryan said, his gaze darting to the boy.

"No worries. Ever since—" The social worker paused and appeared to be carefully considering her words. "For the past week Charlie has been staying with Derek and Rachel Rossi under emergency foster care."

Meg's brows pulled together. "The names sound awfully familiar."

Cole nodded. "I was thinking the same thing."

"Derek is a former major league pitcher," Ryan explained. "He's now an expert sports commentator. So you've probably seen him on TV or at least heard his name. He and his wife, Rachel, live part of the year in Jackson Hole."

"And both of them are friends of your brother Travis and his wife," Lexi added, glancing at Meg. "Rachel has done emergency foster care for years. Charlie has really enjoyed staying at their house."

"I like it there," Charlie agreed. "But I'd rather be with you."

Cole would have liked it better if the boy had been looking only at him when he'd expressed the sentiment. Instead his hope-filled eyes definitely included Meg.

"Soon," Meg said with a reassuring smile.

"We'll be together before you know it," Cole promised.

"It was nice meeting you both." Lexi smiled. "But we should hit the road. I need to get Charlie back to the house. Rachel mentioned something about letting the kids make homemade pizza tonight and—"

"She told me if I came back I could put on the pepperoni." Charlie grabbed Lexi's hand and tugged on it. "We better hurry."

Thankfully, because Charlie was so eager to leave, there were no lingering goodbyes. In a matter of seconds the social worker and the little boy were out the door and down the hall.

Cole assumed Lexi planned it that way, to make it easier on Charlie. Still, it was hard seeing the child disappear from view, knowing he was going to a stranger's home.

Soon, Cole reassured himself. Soon, Charlie would be his. And when that happened he would never let him go.

Chapter Three

"It's good we came when we did." Ryan glanced around the bar. Dressed like Cole in a flannel shirt, jeans and cowboy boots, the successful attorney appeared ready to kick back and relax. "A couple of hours, we'd be lucky to find a place to stand, much less a table."

By the time Cole had reached his late twenties, he'd grown tired of the bar scene. But Wally's Place, a popular Jackson sports bar, had it all: pool, darts, karaoke and, according to Ryan, the best burgers in town.

There was a basket of peanuts on every table and if the rough floor was any indication, tossing the empty shells down was not only acceptable behavior, but encouraged. Their waitress was pretty and more than a little flirtatious, but Cole wasn't interested. He had more important things on his mind tonight.

"What do you think the odds are she'll walk away?"

Cole took a bite of his burger then washed it down with club soda.

"I don't know Margaret well." Ryan took a sip of his Guinness. "In fact, I had to have someone at the funeral point her out to me."

"I feel badly about missing the service," Cole said. Margaret's zinger had hit its target and stuck. "I did everything I could to get here."

"We were supposed to get a dusting." Ryan chuckled. "Instead it was a monster storm. But that's the way this winter has been. Of course, I don't think the weather is any different than it was when you lived here."

A sharp pain shot through Cole's leg. He winced and took another sip of club soda. The way his leg was hurting, he knew he'd have to ice it and pop some pain pills once he got to his hotel room, making alcohol off-limits.

"Of course, give it five minutes and it will change," Ryan said with a good-natured chuckle.

Cole couldn't believe they were discussing the changeable Jackson Hole climate when there were more important issues on the table. He forced a casual tone. "So what do you think of Margaret?"

"'Wow' was the first word that came to my mind, followed quickly by 'hot.'" Ryan shook his head, a tiny smile playing at the corners of his lips. "I can't believe I didn't notice her back in high school."

Cole experienced a twinge of something that felt an awful lot like jealousy—but couldn't have been—at the look in his friend's eyes.

"There were a hundred and fifty kids in our class," Cole reminded him. "She wasn't part of our group."

"But *you* knew her." Ryan returned the smiles of the two young women in tight blue jeans walking past their table, before leveling his gaze back on Cole. "Meg? Isn't that what you called her?"

It had been a slip. He'd been so startled to see her he hadn't been thinking straight. "We may have talked a couple times."

Actually, he and Meg had done a lot more than talk. Until he'd discovered that he couldn't trust her. In a heartbeat she'd gone from being his whole world to being out of his life for good. "What of it?"

"Just that you'd know better than me if she'll back down." Ryan cracked open a peanut and tossed the shell to the floor, all the while keeping his gaze focused on Cole. "What do *you* think? Will she walk away?"

Cole sat back in his seat. He pushed the basket of peanuts closer to Ryan, no longer hungry. "Not a chance in hell."

Two days later, Meg pulled up to the house Cole had rented just outside of Wilson. According to Ryan, Cole had gotten the mountain home fully furnished at a "great deal."

She turned off the ignition of her rental car and took a moment to survey the large two-story stone-and-log structure. Cole must have done well for himself over the years. The "great deals" she'd been looking at in Jackson Hole were a tenth this size, barely inhabitable and a fortune to rent.

Her brother and sister-in-law had told her she and Charlie were welcome to stay with them. It was a generous offer, but Meg worried Charlie would get swallowed up in the chaos of five children under the age of seven. Still, it might be her only option if—

A light tap on the car window pulled Meg from her reverie.

Ryan stood outside the car, wearing a ski cap and parka.

Coupled with his jeans and waterproof hiker boots, he looked more like a college-age ski bum than a successful Jackson Hole attorney. He clapped his gloved hands together as if trying to keep warm, his breath clearly visible in the frigid air.

Meg smiled. Last night Jackson Hole had been blessed with more snow. The ski resort operators were cheering, and having a thick blanket of the white stuff on the ground made her feel like she was truly home.

Ryan motioned with one hand for her to get out of the car.

Slipping her fur-trimmed hood up, Meg pushed the door open and cautiously stepped out. The road to the mountain home had held a hint of a glaze and she wanted to be certain of her footing.

She glanced around but the attorney appeared to be alone.

"You didn't bring Charlie with you?" She couldn't keep the disappointment from her tone.

"We can talk inside." Ryan took her arm as they approached the house, giving her additional stability on the slick sidewalk. "It's freezing out here."

"Wuss," Meg teased until a blast of extra-frigid air hit her face. She picked up her pace and this time it was Ryan's turn to laugh.

"I was looking forward to seeing Charlie." Meg had thought about him often the past couple of days. She'd even considered having Travis invite Rachel and Derek over. In the end she'd decided against the plan, not wanting to do anything that might jeopardize her chance for custody.

"I thought it'd be best if the boy wasn't around when we hashed out the details." Ryan tightened his grip on her arm as they navigated the steps to the front porch.

"You didn't want him traumatized by the yelling and screaming?" Meg said with a wry smile.

"I'm not anticipating any of that." Ryan reached around her to press the doorbell. "You and Cole are rational adults who want only what's best for Charlie. Having you two at each other's throats would only increase the child's stress."

Meg had to grudgingly agree. Although the image of being at Cole's throat did hold a certain appeal.

Meg pressed her hand against her thigh as the wind whipped at her wool skirt. Thankfully she had tights and boots on today as well as a heavy sweater. "I've been looking for an apartment."

Ryan's finger jabbed the doorbell again before casting a curious glance her way. "How's that going?"

"Could be better." Meg wrapped her arms around herself for extra warmth. "Even the dumps are expensive."

The attorney punched the doorbell and chuckled. "Welcome to Jackson Hole."

A brisk breeze slapped Meg in the face. She shivered. "Are you sure Cole is home?"

"I called him on my way here. His knee has really been hurting him." A frown furrowed Ryan's brow. "I hope he didn't fall."

Remembering Cole's unsteady gait and his determination to push his limits back in Ryan's office made losing his balance a definite possibility. Meg's heart picked up speed. "Since he knew we were coming, perhaps he left the door unlocked."

She grasped the ornate door handle with her gloved hand and pushed. It opened easily. A flood of escaping warmth washed over them. She hurried inside with Ryan on her heels.

"Cole, are you okay?" Ryan called out, slipping off his cap and stuffing it into the pocket of his coat.

"Just moving a little slow this morning." Cole hobbled into view on his crutches, the brace on his right knee. He'd ditched the suit he'd been wearing the last time she'd seen him for running pants and a blue long-sleeved cotton shirt.

Meg let out the breath she didn't realize she'd been holding. She told herself her racing heart didn't have a thing to do with him. It was simply that as a rehabilitation professional she saw the signs of a man in considerable pain and facing a long road to recovery.

Slipping off her parka, she placed it in Ryan's outstretched hand before refocusing on Cole. "Have you been doing your exercises?"

"Exercises?" Ryan scoffed. "The guy can barely get around."

"It's important that he starts strengthening his quads right away." Although Margaret now spent her time working primarily with stroke patients, her first job had been at a sports-medicine clinic.

Cole's chin lifted in a defiant tilt. "It's been a busy week."

"I'll take that as a no." Margaret's experienced gaze took in everything from the way Cole was standing to the lines of strain around his eyes. "Do you have a CPM machine?"

"What's that?" Ryan asked Margaret, closing the closet door and picking up the briefcase he'd set on the marble floor.

"Hey, I'm right here," Cole said a bit gruffly. "If you have anything to ask about my rehabilitation, ask me. Why ask her?"

"Because she's the professional," Ryan said.

When Margaret saw the blank look on Cole's face she realized that he had no clue what she did to earn a living, any more than she knew how he could afford a place as expensive as this one.

"I'm a physical therapist," she said. "I've worked with my share of sports injuries. I'm guessing you had an ACL reconstruction. The surgery was somewhere between five and seven days ago—"

"Five." Cole exhaled a breath. "Right before I left to come here."

"And the doctor let you fly?" Margaret didn't even try to keep the surprise from her voice. Most patients were told not to get on a plane for the first two weeks.

"I didn't see another option," Cole said. "I heard the news about Joy and Ty right after I'd gotten out of surgery. I wanted to be here for the funeral. Pay my respects."

His eyes met hers and something unexpected passed between them. She saw her own pain reflected in his and for the first time she realized they shared a common sorrow. In that horrific crash on Route 22, both had lost dear friends.

"I understand," Margaret said softly. Recent surgery wouldn't have kept her away, either. "But I'm sure the doctor emphasized that the first week is the most difficult and a critical time for—"

"He said a lot of things." Cole maneuvered himself into a nearby chair and gestured for them to take a seat. "But we're here today to talk about Charlie and his needs, not mine."

Margaret stepped into the large family room, instantly taking note of the hardwood floor and the number of rugs scattered throughout the room.

Safety hazards. She frowned. If he was her patient, the rugs would all come up until he was steadier on his feet. But he wasn't her patient, so she kept her mouth shut. She contented herself with admiring the rest of the house before taking a seat on a burgundy leather sofa.

From what she could see, the kitchen off to her right held granite countertops and pewter-colored appliances.

Over to her left was a study with French doors, and straight ahead a large stone fireplace with shelves of books on both sides.

Despite being a large home, the place had a surprisingly homey feel. It was easy for Margaret to see Charlie playing with his plastic dinosaurs in front of a roaring fire or running up and down the staircase. Or God forbid, sliding down the banister.

But for Cole and his limitations, this home had to be a nightmare.

"How are you managing the stairs?" The question popped out of Meg's mouth before she could stop it.

"I'm not." Cole repositioned his leg on the ottoman by picking it up and moving it with both hands. "Thankfully everything Charlie and I will need is on this level."

"You're not driving yet." It was a comment, not a question.

"I've found a good car service," Cole said. "Very responsive."

She wondered if he planned to use the car service to transport Charlie to school. Had he even begun to consider any of the dozens of things that had to be done to keep a household running? Duties and tasks which required two fully functioning legs? "I can't imagine how you'll manage—"

"How's the apartment hunting coming?" he asked, cutting her off.

"It's coming." Margaret straightened in her seat and smoothed her plaid skirt with the palm of one hand. "I expect to find a place any day now."

He smiled and it was as if the sun had broken through the clouds. "If anyone will try to make this work it will be you."

A compliment? From Cole? Startled, Margaret wasn't sure how to respond.

Thankfully Ryan stepped into the conversational void.

"We can get into those specifics in a bit." The attorney lifted his briefcase onto the log-and-glass coffee table. "I'd first like to know what your respective attorneys had to say about the enforceability of the joint-custody stipulation in the will."

"Way to jump right in there, Ry." Cole shifted his gaze from Margaret to the attorney. "Before we get started, would either of you like a cup of coffee? Of course, you'll have to get it yourself."

Margaret started to say no but then the deep, rich aroma hit her nostrils. "It smells delicious."

"It's one of our signature blends," Cole said. "Umakka-mecrazy."

Margaret's brows slammed together. "I do what?"

Ryan laughed heartily. "How appropriate."

She cocked her head, feeling as if she'd come late to a party and everyone knew the joke except her. "I don't understand."

"Cole owns Hill of Beans," Ryan explained.

Margaret was familiar with the chain of coffeehouses. There was even one in Omaha, not far from her apartment. She shifted her gaze to Cole. "Is that what you do? Have a franchise in Austin?"

"Something like that," Cole said.

"Actually, he owns the whole company," Ryan said. "Tell her your success story. Local boy makes good and all that."

Cole shot Ryan a warning gaze. "I'm not a trick pony that will perform on command."

"Duly noted," Ryan said, appearing not at all repentant. "Tell her anyway. It'll be a good way to update her on what's been going on with you since high school."

Cole knew his friend too well. Ryan was like a dog with

a bone. He wouldn't move on until he got his way. Cole shifted his gaze to Meg.

"I earned a degree in entrepreneurship from the University of Texas then opened my first coffee shop shortly after graduation," he said matter-of-factly. "We now have forty franchises in seven states."

"But not one in Wyoming," Ryan interjected.

A smile played at the corners of Cole's lips. "Not yet."

Meg's heart dropped. Instead of finding the rags-to-riches story inspiring, all she felt was depressed. And scared. No wonder Cole had attorneys at his disposal and could afford to rent a house like this without batting an eye.

"I think I will take you up on your offer," Ryan said to Cole. "I'd love some coffee."

When the attorney made no move to get up, Meg rose to her feet. "I'll get it."

Cole leaned back in his overstuffed chair like a sovereign on his throne. A rich king who could have anything he wanted...including a little boy who needed a mother.

A little boy who needs me.

The fact that after all these years it took only one look from Cole's baby blues to make her heart skip a beat made Meg even angrier. At herself. At the situation. At him.

"Thank you," he called out when she reached the doorway to the kitchen.

"No thanks necessary." She turned and shot him an imperious gaze. "I don't want to see you fall and have to pick up the pieces."

Pick up the pieces. Like he was some loser who couldn't pull his own weight.

Cole fumed as Meg disappeared into the kitchen, her boots clicking on the hardwood.

He resisted the urge to call her back, to tell her to keep

her hands off his coffee. But that would be childish, so Cole kept his mouth shut and spent the next few minutes listening to Ryan discuss current ski conditions. Not that Cole would be out on the slopes anytime soon.

Still, it beat worrying about how he was going to care for Charlie and wondering what he'd done to make Meg so bitter.

She returned moments later with a tray holding a carafe of coffee and three mugs. It didn't surprise him that she'd remembered to bring the cream and sugar. She'd excelled at anything she'd set her mind to do. Unlike him, who'd struggled through life for years.

When she bent to place the tray on the coffee table, he reluctantly admitted that the plaid skirt and green sweater suited her coloring. He even liked the way she'd pulled her hair to one side with a large tortoiseshell barrette.

Cole glanced down at his shirt and running pants. Ryan had told him the meeting today would be casual. Either Meg hadn't received the message or she'd decided to dress up anyway.

Ignoring his gaze, she filled a cup with the steaming brew then handed it to him, her fingers accidentally brushing against his.

A spark of electricity traveled up Cole's arm. His gaze shot to hers to see if she'd felt it, too. But she'd already turned away to fill Ryan's cup.

By the time she sat down, Cole's leg had begun to throb and all he wanted was to get through the discussion and ice his knee.

"My attorneys say the will is well crafted and completely enforceable." Cole shifted his gaze to Meg. "I assume that's what you discovered, as well."

"Unfortunately yes." Meg's lips pressed together for several heartbeats. "I still can't understand what Joy and Ty were thinking, but it is what it is."

"Which means we'll have to come to a consensus on how to split custody," Cole said. "For now at least."

"For now?" Meg asked.

Cole took a sip of coffee. "Until I discover a way to obtain sole custody."

"I don't understand." Meg placed her cup down with a clatter. "Even your attorneys said the terms of the document are completely enforceable."

"I crafted it carefully," Ryan said in a defensive tone. "There is no way around the stipulations."

"Perhaps." Cole raised the mug to his lips. "But I learned long ago that everything is not always as it appears. Given time I *will* find a way to obtain sole custody. I feel it's in Charlie's best interest to have a single stable home…and I can assure you that home will be with me."

Chapter Four

By the look of shock on Ryan's face, Meg knew the attorney was as stunned as she was by Cole's bold assertion.

"I have to tell you, buddy. I have real concerns about your ability to care for a kid right now." Ryan spoke before she had a chance to respond.

Her spirits rose at the look of shock on Cole's face. Apparently he'd finally remembered the stipulation that gave the attorney the ability to declare either of them unfit.

"If I discover that I need help," Cole said, "I'll hire a live-in nanny to help me until I'm able to care for him by myself."

"You'd bring another new person into Charlie's life?" Ryan's tone made it clear what *he* thought of the idea.

Meg sipped her coffee, waiting to see where the conversation would lead.

"You have a better suggestion? One that doesn't in-volve—" Cole's gaze shifted briefly to Meg "—giving her sole custody?"

Her. As if she didn't have a name. But Meg was too interested in how Ryan would respond to interrupt.

"As a matter of fact, I do." The attorney leaned back in his chair, a smug smile on his face.

"Are you planning to share that suggestion with us?" Cole spoke in a slightly mocking tone.

"Meg moves in with you," Ryan said. "In exchange for free room and board she helps you care for Charlie and does therapy on your knee."

Had Ryan really suggested she and Cole live together? Meg bolted upright in her seat. "No way."

"Absolutely not," Cole echoed.

She exchanged a glance with Cole. She'd never thought this day would come. They finally agreed on something.

"I don't know what happened between the two of you back in high school—"

"Let it go, Ry—" Cole growled.

"—and frankly I don't care." A tiny muscle in Ryan's jaw jumped. "That little boy survived a crash that killed both of his parents. Creating the best possible environment for him to get through this difficult time should take priority over your personal feelings toward each other."

"The house is big enough," Cole murmured as if he was actually considering having her move in with him.

Meg's heart pounded in her ears. She couldn't imagine spending one night in the same house as Cole, much less days or, gulp, weeks.

"I have a place to stay." She spoke quickly, the words tumbling out one after the other as her panic grew. "Charlie can stay with me until—" Meg gestured with one hand toward Cole "—he recovers."

"No." Cole shook his head and his jaw jutted out. "Not happening."

Their momentary truce had taken a sharp detour south.

"Meg." This time it was her turn to be on the receiving end of the attorney's unyielding gaze. "You said you hadn't found an apartment yet. I got the distinct impression money was a major factor."

"Travis and Mary Karen told me I could move in with them." She forced some enthusiasm into her voice. It wasn't easy.

Meg knew if she moved into her brother and sister-in-law's home, Charlie would have an unending supply of playmates. But would he be swallowed up in the chaos? Would she be able to get to know him? To help him heal? Still, to move in with Cole...

She shivered.

"I know Travis and Mary Karen," Ryan said slowly, appearing to choose his words carefully. "They're great people and wonderful parents. But they have five children under the age of seven. Do you really think that's the best environment for Charlie right now?"

Meg had been prepared to argue until he asked the very question that had been troubling her. Still, she couldn't bring herself to say no. She settled for a shrug.

"I'm not suggesting that the two of you live together permanently," Ryan began.

"Thank God," Cole said.

"Just give it a couple months." The attorney fixed his gaze on Cole. "By then you'll each be in a position to care for Charlie on your own or—"

Ryan paused to take a sip of coffee.

"Or?" Meg prompted.

"Or you'll have killed each other."

* * *

The bistro on Scott Lane was crowded with playhouse patrons enjoying post-performance chocolate and espresso while listening to live jazz.

Thankfully, Jackson Hole embraced casual, so Meg didn't feel out of place in her jeans and sweater.

"Are you absolutely sure this is what you want to do?" Travis's eyes were dark with concern.

When her brother had asked her to run into town with him to have some dessert and coffee as a thank-you for the fabulous meal she'd prepared for his family, Meg had immediately agreed.

Since she'd arrived in Jackson last week, she and Travis hadn't had much alone time. His wife must have sensed this, because she'd insisted she wanted to stay home and encouraged Travis to take his sister out.

Meg had been excited, thinking how good it would be to have some one-on-one time with her brother. She'd never considered he might want to revisit her decision to move in with Cole.

"Mary Karen and I would love to have you and Charlie stay with us." Travis's hazel eyes—so like her own—shone with sincerity. "We don't want you to live with Cole because you feel you don't have other options. Because you do. Have other options, I mean."

Meg let her gaze linger on his handsome face. Though his sandy-colored hair was much lighter than hers and he'd inherited a tendency to freckle that she'd somehow managed to escape, their features proclaimed them as brother and sister. It wasn't until Meg had returned to Jackson Hole that she'd realized just how much she missed him.

He was only a year older than her, and when their parents had passed away, it had been the two of them—working as a team—who'd kept the family together.

"Margaret," he said when she didn't answer, pushing his chipotle chocolate pudding to the side and covering her hand with his. "I don't know what happened between you and Cole back in high school but I do know that he hurt you."

"That was a long time ago." Meg took a dainty bite of the French macaroon, preferring to focus on the delicious morsel rather than on the past.

Travis's eyes burned with a protective fire. "Are you saying you've settled things with him?"

Meg didn't want to lie to her brother, but if she said no, she already knew what would happen. He'd *insist* she stay with him.

Not that she didn't love Travis and adore his wife and children, but after spending the past few days in his household, she'd concluded Ryan was right. With one set of six-year-old twin boys, a four-year-old boy and a set of one-year-old twins, her brother's household was very busy. Okay, to a woman used to living alone, it was chaotic. Which meant it was way too crazy for an only child grieving the death of his parents.

"It was high school, Trav." Margaret forced a laugh and waved a dismissive hand. "It'd be pretty sad if I was still holding on to something that happened fifteen years ago. We were just kids."

Travis's eyes searched hers. "If you're sure…"

"Have you ever known me to hold a grudge?" Meg kept her tone light, hoping to dispel the clouds of doubt lingering in her brother's eyes.

The words nearly got caught in her throat but it was worth the effort it took to spit them out when the lines of tension around his eyes eased.

"If he's anything like he used to be, Cole is a good man." As if he'd suddenly rediscovered his appetite, Travis dipped his spoon back into the chocolate pudding he'd been ignoring. "I played ball with him back in high school. He was one of the guys who went out of his way to be nice to Chip."

"Chip" was Christopher Stone, a mentally challenged classmate. He'd been the student assistant for the football and basketball teams during their high school years.

It didn't surprise Meg that Cole had been nice to Chip. He'd always had a soft spot for the underdog. Was that admiration she was feeling? She pushed the feeling aside.

"Whatever happened to Chip?" Meg hadn't thought of her former classmate in years.

"He's a sacker at Hinky Dinky. Appears to enjoy the work." Travis returned the greeting of a very pregnant young woman and her cowboy husband before returning his attention to Meg. "I want to help you move tomorrow. I have surgery in the morning but I can reschedule my afternoon appointments."

"I appreciate the offer, Trav, but all I have is a couple of suitcases." It was true. Even if it wasn't, Travis had done so much for her already. Not only had he opened his home to her, he'd hooked her up with Lexi's attorney husband, Nick, who'd given her free legal advice.

Travis took a bite of pudding then set his spoon down. "What about the rest of your things back in Omaha?"

"Even as we speak, friends are boxing up my clothes and personal items to ship to me." Meg swallowed a sigh. Though it felt good to be "home," there was much about her life in Omaha that she was going to miss.

"It's going to be rough on you for a while since you don't have a paycheck—"

"I also won't have any rent, utility or food costs," she reminded him. She didn't want Travis, or anyone else, feeling sorry for her.

"You'll need spending money." Travis reached into the pocket of his jacket and pulled out an envelope. "Mary Karen and I want you to have this."

Reluctantly, Meg took the plain white envelope from his outstretched hand. She opened it to find a wad of bills stuffed inside. Even as her heart warmed at her brother's generosity, Meg pushed the envelope across the table. "I can't accept this. It's way too generous. You have your own family—"

"You're my family, too." He shoved the envelope back. "I can't tell you how much it means to have you back in Jackson Hole."

"Still—"

"Still nothing." Travis's jaw set in the determined tilt Meg remembered all too well. "Trust me, Mary Karen and I won't even miss it. Consider it an early birthday gift."

Meg rolled her eyes. "We don't exchange gifts."

"We're starting a new tradition," he said with a straight face.

She had to laugh. She knew her big brother and recognized that this was a fight she wasn't going to win. "Okay, I'll take your money. But I'm paying you back."

"Convince even one of our siblings to come home to Jackson Hole and you'll have paid me back a thousand-fold."

Meg started to chuckle but stopped when she saw his face.

"I haven't seen Zac in five years," Travis said, his voice heavy.

"Me, either." Meg shook her head. Of all their siblings, Zac had been the most creative. The most headstrong. And next to Travis, the one she missed the most.

While she couldn't guarantee she'd be able to get one of her brothers and sisters back to Jackson Hole, she'd do her best. Not only for the sake of the man sitting across the table from her, but for her own, as well.

Cole tightened the straps on his knee brace and decided he must have gone crazy. It was the only explanation that made any sense. Why else would he have agreed to let Meg move in?

He slid to the side of the bed and held on to the headboard while pulling himself upright. Catching sight of his reflection in the full-length mirror, he frowned.

While the running pants were comfortable, he felt like he should be going for a jog, rather than entertaining guests.

Not guests, he reminded himself, Meg and Charlie. While Meg might be considered a guest, Charlie was definitely family.

"My son," Cole whispered the words aloud for the first time, the taste sweet against his tongue.

For the past five years, ever since he'd heard Joy had given birth less than nine months after their fling in Austin, he'd wondered if Charlie was his son.

By the time he'd heard the news, Joy was married to Ty. Still, Cole had contacted her. She'd insisted the baby was her husband's child, but her words—and the timing—didn't ring true. When he'd suggested they do a DNA test "just to be sure," Joy had started to cry.

At that point Cole had let the matter drop. After all, he didn't know for sure. And, in the eyes of the law, Charlie was considered Ty's son. Not only that, Ty was a good father and he and Joy were happy together. In the ensuing years, Cole had become a friend to Ty as well as to Joy and a favorite "uncle" to Charlie.

But now everything had changed.

Grabbing his crutches, Cole made his way slowly to the

living room to await Charlie and Meg's arrival. He stifled a groan as he eased into the overstuffed leather chair. The time for making excuses was over. Once Charlie was settled in, he'd start hitting the therapy hard. And he wouldn't need Meg's help. No sirree.

He couldn't believe he and Meg would be living under the same roof. It was like some twisted fairy tale. To think there had been a time when he'd have given anything to have her be the last person he saw at night and the first one when he woke up. That, of course, was before he discovered she couldn't be trusted.

The ringing of the doorbell saved Cole from revisiting that awful time when he'd learned she'd betrayed him. The melodious chimes had launched into a second refrain by the time he made it to his feet.

He hobbled around the furniture, carefully avoiding the treacherous rugs. Excitement built inside Cole. Having the opportunity to be a father to Charlie was a dream come true.

Still, it had come at a high price.

Too high, Cole thought grimly. Joy and Ty had been like family—closer, really, than his own brother—and he felt their loss to the very core of his being.

He'd made it all the way to the edge of the foyer when the door opened and Meg and Charlie spilled inside, laughing and talking.

"I hope you don't mind us not waiting." Meg stomped on the rag rug, sending the snow on her boots flying across the marble floor. Tiny flakes of white ice crystals clung to her hair.

"I was c-c-cold," Charlie said loudly, whipping off his Denver Broncos ski cap, his hair standing straight up. "I could see my breath and everything. If I'd waited much longer I'd 'ave froze to death."

The little boy's expression was so earnest, Cole swallowed the laughter welling in his throat.

"Couldn't have that." Cole gestured to the coat closet off to Meg's left. "If you'd like to hang up your—"

"I'd better keep mine on." She slanted a glance at Charlie. "We've got some bags. I should bring them in before my car is covered with snow."

"There's a garage door opener on the side table," Cole said. "It's yours while you're here."

A garage door opener. A simple tool, nothing more. Then why did it suddenly feel so…intimate?

If it felt intimate to Meg, she gave no indication. She simply grabbed the control, dropped it into her pocket then turned to Charlie, who was unbuttoning his jacket.

"Leave it on, sweetie," she said to the boy. "I'm going to need help carrying the bags into the house."

"I don't want to carry any dumb old bags," the boy whined. "I wanna see my room."

"You can see your room," Cole answered before Meg could respond, "*after* you help Aunt Meg."

Charlie's face took on a mulish look. He opened his mouth as if to speak, but closed it when Cole shot him a firm glance.

"Okay," the boy said with a huge sigh.

"Thank you, Charlie," Meg added. "I appreciate the help."

"Is there anything I can do?" Cole asked Meg.

"Thanks for offering, but we'll be able to manage." For a second her smile was open and friendly. "Look at Charlie's muscles."

Beside her, the boy puffed with pride. "I'm real strong. I picked up this big punkin from our garden that even Daddy couldn't lift."

The sharp pain of loss sliced through Cole's heart. As

much as he'd wanted to take a bigger role in Charlie's life, he'd never wanted it to come at Ty's expense.

"Daddy and me put a mean face on it," the boy continued. "Mommy got scared when we showed it to her."

"Your mommy told me that story," Meg responded with a smile, smoothing the child's hair.

Cole wondered if Meg realized how therapeutic her talking about Joy and Ty was for Charlie. When Cole's father passed away, his mom had made it clear he and his brother weren't to talk about their dad or even mention his name. Cole had never been sure if that was because her husband's death was so hard on her or if she just didn't want to upset her new boyfriend.

"Charlie, honey, you stay in here until you hear me honk. That will be your signal to come and help me. Understand?"

The boy nodded.

With an ease that Cole couldn't help envying, Meg slipped out the front door, pulling it closed behind her.

Charlie met Cole's gaze. "Aunt Margaret and me got my toys and clothes. My mommy and daddy's stuff was all gone."

The pain and confusion in the child's voice tugged at Cole's heartstrings. Not responding wasn't an option. Not with those big blue eyes focused on him, searching for answers.

"My daddy died when I wasn't much older than you." Cole cleared his throat. "Before long, everything of his was gone from our home. It felt as if he'd never been there."

"Did it make you feel sad?" Charlie asked in a small voice.

"It did," Cole agreed. "But then I realized his clothes and fishing and hunting gear were just things. My dad was still with me. He'd always be with me. Understand?"

Charlie's face scrunched up in a frown. "I guess."

Cole decided to further simplify. "My dad was sick for almost a year before he died. We all knew it wouldn't be long before he'd go to heaven."

"Did you tell him not to go?" Charlie's bottom lip trembled. "Did you tell him that you'd miss him? That you were scared to be alone?"

Cole pressed his lips together, remembering just how alone and scared he'd felt. His dad had been the only person he'd been able to count on. "Before he passed on, he told me that wherever I went, he'd be in my back pocket. Understand?"

Charlie's brows pulled together for a long moment, then he nodded.

Cole expelled a breath.

The boy patted the back pocket of his jeans and a look of confusion blanketed his face. "I don't feel Daddy here."

"He's not actually—" Cole stopped when Charlie squealed with laughter.

"I fooled you." A big grin split the boy's face.

The faint honking of a car horn broke through the laughter.

"I gotta go." Charlie spun around and took off in the direction of the front door.

"Not that way. The door to the garage is through there." Cole gestured with his head in the direction of the kitchen.

"I'm coming," Charlie said in a loud voice, though there was no way she could hear him. "I'm coming, Aunt Margaret."

Cole waited until the child disappeared into the kitchen before he returned to the chair he'd vacated minutes before.

Aunt Margaret.

Uncle Cole.

To an outsider, it probably sounded as if they were a family. As if they belonged together.

But they were living together for only one reason. As soon as he was on his feet, she'd be shown the door.

And once he got full custody, she'd be out of his life.

This time for good.

Chapter Five

The evening sped by quickly. Remembering that Joy had told her spaghetti was Charlie's favorite dish, Meg had swung by the grocery store before picking up the boy.

Cole had seemed as pleased as Charlie when she'd announced what they were having for dinner. Seeing his empty cupboards and refrigerator, she understood.

In an attempt to provide a balanced meal, Meg made steamed broccoli for the vegetable and strawberries with whipped cream for dessert. By the time she and Charlie cleared the table, a tiny bit of the tension between her and Cole had eased.

Cole's eyes might still be shuttered but he'd smiled a couple of times. Not that she cared for herself what the man thought or felt. But at least she knew he wanted things to be comfortable between them…for the child's sake.

She sent Charlie to the living room to keep Cole company while she wiped down the granite countertops. Meg ran her fingers across the surface, her gaze surveying the room.

The commercial-grade appliances were every cook's dream. Growing up in a big family, helping in the kitchen was just something you were expected to do. Later, after her parents had passed away, and she and Travis had chosen to take on the daunting task of coparenting their siblings, she'd been grateful for all those lessons. But her uncle's kitchen had been nothing like this one.

"Aunt Meg," Charlie called out from the other room. "Where are you?"

"Aunt Meg?" She strolled into the room, not sure how she felt about seeing the boy sitting so comfortably beside Cole on the sofa. Especially with his head cocked in a gesture that reminded her of the man sitting beside him. "What happened to Aunt Margaret?"

"Meg is more pretty," the boy said with a decisive nod. "It's what Uncle Cole calls you."

Meg shifted her gaze.

Cole's lips lifted upward in a smile that looked suspiciously like a smirk. "You're welcome."

She'd been about to suggest they play one of the board games she'd brought with her from Charlie's house or perhaps a rousing hand of Go Fish. But the smirk changed the direction of her thoughts.

"Charlie," she said. "Would you like to help me make your uncle Cole strong and fast, like a superhero?"

"Yes," Charlie shouted, jumping to his feet and pumping his fist in the air.

"Indoor voice." Meg touched a finger to her lips, smiling to soften the words.

"Will he be able to fly?" Charlie flung out his arms as if he were prepared to soar through the air.

"No, he won't be able to fly but eventually he will be

able to take you skiing and then fishing this summer." Meg kicked the crutches Cole had propped up next to him on the sofa. "He'll be able to walk and run without these."

Cole's expression darkened.

"How are we gonna make him strong?" Charlie asked.

"Through some fun games," Meg said. "It's very important that these games are done just right. That's why I'll be the sheriff and you'll be the deputy. We're here to make sure he does just what the doctor ordered."

"Do I get a gun?" the boy asked.

Meg shook her head. "A gun won't be necessary."

"My daddy had a gun. I wasn't allowed to touch it. He kept it locked up in a big cabinet."

"Well," Meg said, "there are no guns here—"

She glanced at Cole for confirmation.

"No guns," he said.

"And we don't need them," Meg said. "Because Uncle Cole wants to get better and because of that he's going to do what we say."

"I don't think—" Cole began.

"If he cheats, I'll arrest him," Charlie announced, his expression stern. "Cuz I want him to take me fishing. I don't know about skiing. I never been."

"You'll like it," Cole said. "I'll take you when my knee is healed."

"I want Aunt Meg to come, too." Charlie reached out and took her hand, the gesture warming her heart.

"Then I'd better start getting in shape," Cole drawled.

"I can help with that," Meg said.

"I see that look in your eyes," Cole said. "What do you have in mind, Aunt Meg?"

"Your CPM machine," she said, not at all affected by his easy smile. "Where is it?"

"In my bedroom." Cole gestured toward the hall with his head.

In Meg's experience, a continuous-passive-motion machine was often prescribed for use during the first two weeks after an ACL reconstruction.

"Have you used it today?" she asked.

"I was busy." His tone held a defensive edge. "Getting things ready for you and Charlie."

Meg wasn't sure that Cole was physically capable of doing much to ready the house for their arrival, but she let the topic drop.

"What degree of extension does the doctor want you to achieve before you discontinue the use of the CPM?" Meg kept her tone professional and her comment to the point.

"Ninety-five," he said.

"I'll get it for you."

"I'm almost at ninety-five," he called to her retreating back.

Meg kept walking. The awkwardness of his gait told her he still had a way to go. Only when she reached his bedroom door did indecision strike. She really should have secured his permission before entering his personal space.

Of course, since he wasn't yelling for her to return or telling her to stay out, apparently he was okay with her retrieving the equipment. Right?

Pushing open the bedroom door, her breath caught in her throat. Bedroom? More like a suite. A sizable sitting area done in burgundy and grays held a love seat, an easy chair and an end table. A flat-screen television was mounted on one wall. The step up to the king-size bed was aesthetically pleasing but probably a hassle to Cole in his current condition. She took note of the CPM machine next to the bed but passed by it, not ready to stop exploring.

Off to the right was a bathroom with a glassed-in shower and a separate alcove with a tub the size of a Jacuzzi.

Cole's razor and shaving cream were on the bathroom counter between double sinks. A burgundy towel hung drying on a silver towel bar.

A manly mixture of cologne and soap and shaving cream lingered in the air. Meg could see Cole standing in front of the mirror clad in nothing but a towel, beads of moisture clinging to his muscular chest.

For a second she was back in his old Chevy, tentatively sliding her hands up under his shirt, exploring those muscles with the pads of her fingers.

An unexpected ache of longing washed over her, shocking her with its intensity. The intimacy they'd shared in the vehicle's backseat had been her first, and if his awkwardness had been an indication, his, as well. It made no sense that the long-ago encounter that night had become the gold standard.

Though Meg hadn't had many lovers since, she'd had a couple. Both were experienced men. Neither one had sent fire rushing through her veins with a single touch. Or brought her to completion that left her breathless and longing for more.

Meg took a deep breath, banished the memory to the past where it belonged and turned back to the bedroom area, to the equipment propped up beside the headboard. She gathered it in her arms, finding the item more unwieldy than heavy.

When she reached the living room Charlie was teaching Cole a song about monkeys jumping on a bed. Charlie stopped singing when he saw her and raced across the room.

"Aunt Meg, I lighted the fire all by myself." With a big

grin splitting his face, the boy pointed to the hearth where a fire now burned.

She glanced at Cole and raised a brow. Surely he knew that Charlie was much too young to be playing with matches.

Cole smiled as if he could read her mind. "Tell Aunt Meg what you used to start the fire."

The boy picked up a tan-colored remote control from the side table. "This."

Of course. A gas log. Energy efficient. Clean. Most of all, so safe a child could "fire" it up.

"It's nice and—" her word faltered as she caught Cole staring "—warm in here now."

Warm wasn't really the word that sprang to mind. Intimate. Cozy. Perhaps even a bit seductive.

Between the crackling fire and the falling snow visible through the floor-to-ceiling windows, there was a feeling of closeness that Meg hadn't expected to experience here.

Charlie pointed to the equipment in her arms. "What's that?"

The boy moved close, touched a finger to the metal. He jumped back as if it was red-hot then giggled.

Meg smiled at the boyish antics. She turned to place the item on the floor by the sofa. "This is going to help make Uncle Cole strong again."

"It looks hard." Charlie's face scrunched into a frown as Meg placed the CPM machine on the floor.

"It *is* hard," Cole agreed. "Can I count on you to help me?"

"Yes, sir." Charlie nodded vigorously up and down then slanted a glance at Meg before turning back to Cole. "You can count on both of us."

"Is that right, Meg?" Cole lifted a sardonic brow. "Can I count on you...this time?"

The words stung as much as if he'd slapped her. Yet, for Charlie's sake, she managed to keep a smile on her lips.

The nerve of the man. He acted as if it was *her* who'd let him down all those years ago rather than the other way around.

Snapping the last piece of the equipment into place, Meg scrambled to her feet and held out a hand to him. She met his gaze. "Of course you can trust me, Cole. Every bit as much as I can trust you."

Cole saw the anger in her eyes, heard it in the bite of her tone. Too subtle for Charlie to catch; nevertheless the exchange had brought a chill to the room that no fire could warm.

Though he wanted to tell her that they both knew she was the one who couldn't be trusted, he kept his mouth shut. He remembered all too well how hard it had been for him as a child to listen to his mom bicker with her new husband.

There was a child in the house. This meant any animosity between him and Meg had to be put to bed. At the very least while Meg was living under his roof and probably until he could sever her custody ties with Charlie.

It wasn't fair for the boy to be put in the middle of adult business. Besides, what happened between Meg and him had been a lifetime ago. While it was doubtful he'd ever trust her again, they were two adults. For Charlie's sake they should be able to put the past behind them. Which meant no sniping at each other.

"Uncle Cole." Once again at his side, Charlie tugged on his sweater. "Aren't you going to take Aunt Meg's hand? She's had it out there a long time."

"Worried I'll let you fall?" she softly taunted, a smile on her lips.

"Not in the least." Cole closed his fingers around Meg's, disturbed by the intensity of emotions the touch aroused.

He met her gaze. Despite his earlier gibe, he wasn't worried she'd let him fall. From what he'd seen, she was too much of a professional to let personal feelings influence her job performance.

In less than a minute Cole was settled on the floor, strapped into the machine, feeling it work its magic.

Meg, with some enthusiastic help from Charlie, had propped him up with pillows against the back of the sofa.

"Now what?" Charlie asked.

Cole opened his mouth to suggest they watch the basketball game on television, but stopped himself just in time. This was his son's first night with him. He couldn't believe he'd considered television even for a moment.

"Can we watch TV?" Charlie asked, plopping down on the floor beside him.

Cole swallowed a chuckle at Meg's look of shock.

"I thought tonight might be a good chance for the three of us to get better acquainted," she said diplomatically.

"What did you have in mind?" Cole tried to keep the suspicion from his voice. While he'd never been a holding-hands-around-the-campfire kind of guy, he wanted to keep an open mind.

Charlie's brows pulled together. "I don't know what *akwadented* means."

"It means," Meg said, settling into a nearby chair, "that we get to know each other better by asking and answering the same questions about each other."

"I dunno," Charlie said, his expression uncertain.

Cole glanced longingly at the fifty-two-inch television. The basketball game was looking better by the second.

"For example," Meg said, apparently not dissuaded by

their lack of enthusiasm, "my favorite color is green. What's yours?"

Charlie shrugged.

The look on Meg's face fell. Cole knew he could squash this game with a few well-chosen words. But that would be mean. Plus he'd vowed to keep an open mind. He forced some excitement into his voice. "Mine is blue."

"That's my favorite color, too," Charlie said.

"See, isn't this fun?" Meg asked. The smile remained on her lips but he heard the strain in her voice, saw it on her face.

Charlie looked at Cole.

"It's a lot of fun," Cole said.

"It's fun," the little boy echoed.

Cole grinned. That was his boy.

Meg sighed.

"Let's stick with the basics for a little bit," Meg said, then proceeded over the next thirty minutes to ferret out their favorite food, their favorite pet—they all liked dogs best—even their favorite thing to do in the evening.

When Charlie said sitting on his daddy's lap while listening to him read *The Poky Little Puppy* was his "most favoritist thing in all the world," Cole's throat clogged up.

"You had a nice daddy," Meg said. "I had a nice daddy, too."

Unexpectedly she shifted her gaze to Cole. "How about you?"

"He was great."

"Looks like we were all blessed with wonderful fathers," Meg said softly.

"Did your daddy read you *The Poky Little Puppy?*" Charlie asked Cole.

"I don't remember." Okay, it wasn't a truthful answer but if he said no, Charlie would surely ask why. There was no way Cole wanted to get into his father's reading difficulties.

"I think it's time to unhook Uncle Cole from the machine." Meg slanted a glance in Charlie's direction. "Want to help, deputy?"

The boy's somber expression immediately brightened. He pumped a fist in the air.

Cole braced himself when Charlie jumped to his feet. But he'd taken only a few steps when Meg reached out and laid a restraining hand on the boy's arm.

"It's important to be gentle." Her tone was soft but firm. "Understand?"

Charlie nodded. "I can, I can be gentle."

Cole released the breath he'd been holding as Meg patiently showed the boy how to release the straps.

"I do it," the boy said loudly after Meg's demonstration.

"Show me," Meg said.

With his tongue between his teeth, Charlie carefully unhooked the straps one by one while Cole murmured encouragement.

Once he was finished, Charlie threw his hands up like a wrestler who'd just pinned an opponent. "Yes."

Meg clapped him on the back. "Fabulous job, deputy."

"I did good, didn't I, Uncle Cole?" Charlie's voice quivered.

Meg had made it clear she thought the boy had done a good job, yet it was Cole's approval Charlie sought.

"You did indeed." Cole reached up and ruffled the child's hair, pride flowing through his veins like an awakened river.

Still, when it came time for the brace to go back on his knee, Cole wasn't sorry that it was Meg's competent hands that helped him put it on and held out a steadying hand as he rose to his feet.

"That was fun, Aunt Meg." Charlie leaned in close. "Can I help again?"

"Absolutely," she said.

Cole glanced at Charlie's beaming face. He thought of all he'd learned tonight about his son. And all that Charlie had learned about him. That never would have happened if they'd been watching a basketball game.

"Thank you," he said to Meg when Charlie ran to the bathroom.

"For helping you up?"

"No," he said. "For making the evening…nice."

A look of shock flickered in her eyes before she shrugged. "It was important to me that he had a good first night here."

"Well, I appreciate it," he said, surprised by the admiration flowing through his veins. Cole didn't want to have these feelings for her, didn't want to feel the bar between them lower by even the slightest inch.

But he told himself there was no need to worry. He'd let down his guard once before with her and had gotten burned. He wouldn't be making that mistake again.

Chapter Six

The ringing of her cell phone woke Meg from a sound sleep. She fumbled with the bedcovers, reaching blindly for the phone charging on the bedside stand.

"Margaret."

"Zac?" Meg jerked upright, instantly wide-awake at hearing her brother's voice. "What time is it?"

"Two."

"Two o'clock in the morning?" She squeaked, tightening her fingers around the phone. "Is something wrong?"

"Nothing is wrong." He chuckled. "Can't a guy call his sister to see how she's doing without it being some problem?"

But not in the middle of the night.

The words never made it to Meg's lips. Zac called so rarely that she'd gladly take his calls no matter what the time of the day or night. She smiled into the phone. "It's good to hear your voice, bro."

"I heard that you're back in Jackson, playing house with some guy. True? Or false?"

Sheesh. She'd just moved in today. "Did Trav tell you that?"

"I haven't spoken with him," Zac said in a tone that gave nothing away. "Is it true? Are you shacking up?"

"You tell me your secrets and I'll tell you mine." Meg wasn't sure why she was toying with him. She certainly didn't want him thinking she and Cole meant anything to each other.

"What do you want to know?" he asked, sounding amused.

"Where you are would be a good place to start."

"Wichita."

"Kansas?" Meg couldn't hide her surprise. Her youngest brother had always been more of a big-city guy.

"I met a girl," he said.

A girl. With his dark hair and gray eyes, Zac attracted women in droves. "Is it serious?"

"More complicated than serious."

"Will you be staying in Wichita?"

"I can work anywhere," he said, not really answering her question. Meg had never been sure what her brother did for a living, other than it involved welding.

"Enough about me." His tone made it clear he'd tolerate no more questions. "Let's talk about you."

"What do you want to know?"

"I hear you've got a kid now."

"Your sources are correct." With one hand, Meg propped some pillows behind her and settled back against the fluffy softness. "You remember my friend Joy? Well, she and her husband were killed on that same stretch of road where Mom and Dad died. Their wish was that Cole Lassiter and I would share joint custody of their son, Charlie. He's six."

"Since you three are together, I take it you agreed."

"He's a child, Zac." Meg found herself softening her tone, just thinking of the boy. "He needs me."

"Raising a kid is a big commitment," he said in a subdued tone. "A lot of people would walk away."

"Who, Zac? Who would do that? Not me. Certainly not you."

Growing up, her youngest brother—now twenty-six years old—may have been hell on wheels, but he had a good heart.

"I suppose you're right."

Meg heard something in the background. A cat crying? Or was it a baby? "What's that noise?"

"Look, I gotta go. I'll be in touch."

Before Meg could say another word, he'd hung up.

Meg stared at the phone for several seconds then put the phone back on the charger.

First Cole saying thank-you. Now her baby brother calling out of the blue.

She snuggled back against the pillow, eager to see what tomorrow would bring. Because everyone knew that good things came in threes...

Cole opened his eyes to sunlight streaming in through the windows and the smell of bacon in the air. Instead of immediately getting up and investigating, he took a few minutes to do some of the exercises he'd been given back in Austin.

Hearing the excitement in Charlie's voice when he'd talked about them skiing and fishing made Cole eager to get back to full speed sooner rather than later. Though the exercises weren't pleasant, he knew he was making progress. That meant someday soon he'd be able to take care of his son all by himself.

His son.

The kit for checking his and Charlie's DNA should arrive in the mail any day. If the tests showed that he was the child's biological father, obtaining sole custody would be that much easier. But even if the tests showed it wasn't his blood flowing through the little boy's veins, Cole would love him just as much and be proud to call him son.

A hesitant knock sounded at the door. Cole flung a sheet over himself. "Come in."

A second later, Charlie slipped inside the room. "Are you awake? Aunt Meg said I wasn't supposed to wake you."

"I'm awake." Cole motioned the boy closer, noticing he was already dressed for the day in jeans, boots and a long-sleeved cowboy shirt. "Looks like you've been up awhile."

Charlie nodded, stopping when he reached the end of the bed. "I'm going to a birthday party. We're going to have cake 'n' ice cream and go on a ride in a sleigh and everything."

"Sounds like a fun party," Cole said, amazed by the boy's enthusiasm. "Who's having the birthday?"

"My friend Jake. He's in my grade at school. He's seven."

Cole hid a smile at the awe in Charlie's voice. "Getting old."

"I'm six," Charlie said. "I'll be seven at my next birthday."

"Charlie." Meg's voice sounded from the hall. "I thought I told you not to wake him up."

"I was already awake," Cole said. "I'd even done my exercises."

Meg pushed the door fully open and stepped inside. Like Charlie, she wore jeans and boots. But that was where any similarity ended. Her green sweater brought out the color in her eyes and the lushness of her figure.

Back in high school she'd worn loose sweaters to conceal her rather sizable…assets. When they'd made love, he'd been shocked—and pleased—to discover what she'd been hiding under those baggy shirts.

"Cole."

He jerked his gaze up from her chest to find her staring. "Do you want to ride along when I take Charlie into Jackson for his party?"

"Sure," he said, surprised at the invitation. Perhaps he wasn't the only one who'd resolved to be civil. "What are we going to do while he's at the party?"

"Grocery shopping," she said in a matter-of-fact tone. "I checked out the kitchen and the cupboards are bare."

Cole couldn't argue with that assessment. He'd planned to stock up on food before Charlie and Meg arrived but had run out of time. "Sure. It'll be good to get out of the house."

Meg hesitated, as if suddenly struck with second thoughts. "If you're sure you have the stamina?"

Cole wondered if she really was concerned about his stamina or if she hated to spend that much time with him. He hoped it was the former because over the next few weeks they were going to be together constantly.

"I'm up for it." He sniffed the air and his stomach growled. "I assume we'll be eating before we leave?"

"The bacon got to you, huh?" Her lips lifted in a friendly smile. "I swear my brothers could smell bacon from a block away."

"Do you have any left?" he asked, trying not to sound too eager.

"You bet." She shifted her gaze to the little boy, who now sat on the edge of the bed swinging his legs. "Actually I was looking for Charlie to tell him that breakfast was ready when I heard your voices."

Charlie raised his hand as if he was in school but didn't

wait to be recognized. "We're havin' bacon 'n' eggs and milk and juice and—"

Meg placed a hand on Charlie's shoulder. "Honey, why don't you wash your hands and then you can help me set the table."

"'Kay." The boy hopped off the bed and galloped from the room.

"Cole?" His name sounded strangled coming from her lips.

"Yes?"

"Put some clothes on, please."

He wasn't sure why she'd mentioned it until he glanced down. The sheet he'd tossed over his bare body rode low on his abdomen. Another couple of inches and he'd have given her quite a show.

Cole smiled, recalling a time when that wouldn't have been an issue. "I'll show you mine if you show me yours," had been said more than once as things had heated up between them. Until one night, she'd unbuttoned her shirt. And he'd unzipped his pants.

He looked up at the sound of the door clicking shut behind her. Cole expelled a harsh breath and reached for the brace beside the bed. Those days of playful banter and lustful thoughts were long gone.

All he cared about now was getting stronger so he could take care of Charlie on his own.

He glanced down. Too bad his body hadn't gotten that message yet.

Charlie came out of the bathroom, hands still dripping water, eager to set the table.

Meg took the Fiesta dinnerware from the cupboard and placed it on the counter where Charlie could easily reach it.

"Your face is red." The little boy picked up a bright orange plate and stared into it as if trying to see his reflection. "Are you hot?"

"A little." Actually, Meg found herself in the uncomfortable position of fighting off a surge of lust. You'd think it had been decades instead of a little over a year since she'd seen a man naked.

Granted, Cole hadn't been completely uncovered but that sheet had dipped precariously low. His muscular chest and washboard abs told her he hadn't been sitting around eating Cheetos and watching television all his life.

"I'm not hot." Charlie laid the plate carefully on the table. "And I'm not cold. I'm just right."

The way he changed the pitch of his voice reminded Meg of Goldilocks at the home of the three bears. But his face was serious so she bit back her laughter.

She knew there would be times when Charlie would be sad, but the way he'd begun to adjust told her that moving in with her and Cole had been the best thing for the boy.

So, if being here meant putting up with the man who'd once broken her heart, it was a small price to pay.

The grocery store parking lot seemed surprisingly empty for the Saturday before Christmas. Meg glanced at the clock on the dash of Cole's SUV. "We have an hour before we need to pick up Charlie."

Cole slanted a sideways glance in her direction. "He seemed happy this morning."

"I thought so, too." Unbuckling her seat belt, Meg pushed open the door then turned back to him. "Are you sure you're going to be okay without your crutches?"

When they'd left the house, Cole had insisted on leaving his walking aids behind, asserting it had been two weeks now and it was time to move on.

"I'm good." He turned toward the door, his brow pulled together in concentration as he eased himself out of the passenger side.

The grocery store parking lot had been bladed, but snow still crunched under Meg's boots when she stepped onto the pavement. She put on her physical therapist's hat and her experienced gaze turned sharp and assessing.

The slippery path to the brightly lit store entrance was an accident waiting to happen. One fall would undo all the work the surgeon had done to reconstruct Cole's ACL.

Meg hurried around the front of the truck and took his arm just as he shut his door.

He glanced down at the arm which now held him tight then lifted his gaze back to her face, a smirk on his lips. "Why, Meg, darlin', I didn't know you cared."

"I don't, Cole, sweetheart," she said in the same phony Southern drawl. "But if you fall on your as—ah, backside, it will impact not only Charlie's quality of life, but mine, as well. I'm simply making sure that doesn't happen."

She swore he chuckled. All she cared was that he didn't protest as they made their way across the lot. Strangely, while holding on to the arm of a man she didn't care about—at all—she felt like part of a couple. Which was crazy for so many reasons, but most of all she couldn't recall ever feeling this close to him, not even when they'd been seeing each other.

"Do you realize," she said when the treacherous trek ended and the automatic doors slid open in welcome, "that even when we were dating, I never held your hand or took your arm?"

"That's because," he said, "you wouldn't allow it. You didn't want anyone to know you were dating me. Especially not any of your Honor Society pals."

For a second Meg was struck dumb by the hint of bitterness underscoring his words. "That's not how it was at all," she protested when she finally found her voice. "You—"

"Meg. Cole. What a nice surprise."

Meg whirled.

Lexi Delacourt, social worker extraordinaire, looking absolutely lovely in navy leggings and a bulky navy-and-white cable-knit sweater, stood next to a cart filled with sacks of groceries, her husband, Nick, at her side. "I didn't expect to see you here."

The curious look in both their eyes told Meg it wasn't seeing her that was such a surprise, but seeing her holding on to Cole.

"There was no food in the house." Meg released her grip on his arm as if it were a hot potato.

"It was either brave the grocery store aisles or starve." Cole's curious gaze settled on Nick.

"Where are my manners?" Lexi said with a little laugh. "Meg has met my husband, but you haven't."

The pretty social worker made quick work of the introductions.

"A family-law attorney," Cole said after he and Nick had shaken hands. He cast a quick glance at Meg before returning his attention to Nick. "I bet you found the provisions of Joy and Ty's will very interesting."

Meg's heart sank to the tips of her boots. *He knew.* Somehow without her saying a word, Cole *knew* Nick was the attorney she'd consulted about the will.

"My wife doesn't discuss her cases with me," Nick said, an easy smile on his lips.

"Lexi may not, but I did." Meg lifted her chin. She had nothing to hide. "Nick verified the provisions were completely enforceable."

Instead of offering up his normal remark to the tune of "we'll see about that," Cole simply smiled.

"Mary Karen tells me the two of you are living together." Lexi's eyes were bright with interest.

"Living in the same house," Cole clarified.

"Not together, together." Meg's cheeks burned as Cole's lips twitched.

"What Meg is trying to say is—" he paused to place a hand on her shoulder "—we're not sleeping together."

"Not yet anyway," Lexi said with a devilish gleam in her eyes.

Nick chuckled. "You'll have to excuse my wife. She has the soul of a matchmaker."

For a second Meg was tempted to make it clear that Cole Lassiter would be the last man on earth she'd ever sleep with, or—she shuddered—to marry, but she stopped the words before they made it past her lips.

How many times had she told her younger siblings that there was no excuse for mean-spiritedness? Besides, she'd learned long ago there was danger in protesting too much.

Meg gestured to Lexi's shopping cart. "Looks like you're getting ready to do it up big for Christmas."

"We're not always in Jackson Hole for the holidays, so we're going all out and having everyone over next Saturday night," Nick said.

"Nick and Lexi live part of the year in Dallas," Meg explained to Cole.

"Although I grew up here, I've spent the past fourteen years in Texas," Cole said to Nick. "My business holdings are based out of Austin."

"Great town." Nick nodded approvingly. "The live music scene is awesome."

While the two men launched into a discussion of all things Texas, Lexi pulled Meg aside.

"How's it going? And be honest. I was stunned when I heard the news—"

"It's okay," Meg said, realizing it was true. Yes, considering their past, being thrust into such close proximity was a bit awkward, but so far Cole had been a gentleman.

He'd praised her cooking, had encouraged Charlie to help her carry bags inside and had even supported her "getting to know you" game last night. "We're figuring it out."

"Lex, not to break this up, but we did tell Coraline we'd pick up the children—" Nick held up his smart phone so his wife could see the time "—in five minutes."

"Yikes, I didn't realize it was this late." The look Lexi shot Meg was filled with regret. "Coraline runs a B and B and does all the cooking, so she'll need to get supper started. Addie, our oldest, is a good little helper, but Grace is a toddler and into everything."

"We need to rush, too," Meg said. "Charlie is at a birthday party and we'll have to pick him up before long."

"Do you have any plans for the holidays?" Lexi asked, her gaze widening to include Cole.

"I haven't even thought about it," Cole said. "Right now I've been just taking it day by day."

"Well—" Lexi glanced at her husband, who gave her a barely perceptible nod "—we'd love it if you'd celebrate with us next Saturday. It's always a good time when everyone gets together. Travis and Mary Karen will be there, and David and July. Derek and Rachel are in town, so they'll come. As well as a few single friends. And all the children, of course. We're planning on eating at six."

This must be the party Travis had mentioned. Of course, he'd offered to cancel, saying he'd love to spend more time with her.

At the time, things had been in such an upheaval, making plans for the Saturday prior to Christmas had been the furthest thing from her mind. Unfortunately, now the holiday was less than a week away.

"If you plan to settle in Jackson Hole, it would be a good way to get acquainted," Nick said with a warm smile.

Meg cast a sideways glance at Cole. He appeared receptive to the idea but this was something they should discuss privately.

"Thank you so much for the generous offer," Meg said. "Can we get back to you later today?"

"No rush," Lexi said. "Anytime this week is fine. And if you decide to come, don't worry about bringing anything. We've got the food completely covered."

Once they were alone, Cole turned to her. "Why did you say we'd get back to them? Why didn't you just accept?"

"Because you and I needed to discuss the offer." Meg carefully placed apples into a plastic bag then twist tied it shut and handed it to Cole to place in the cart.

"I'd have gone along with whatever you decided."

"Thank you for that," Meg said. "But I believe that parenting is a joint effort. When Travis and I were helping raise our siblings, we discovered early on the importance of not only being on the same page but of presenting a united front."

"My mom and dad didn't operate that way." He grabbed a head of lettuce and dunked it into the cart with a high lob. "And my stepdad and my mom were too busy bickering to think of anything else."

Meg hadn't known much about Cole's home life back in their high school days. Oh, she'd heard the gossip. How his mom had remarried less than six weeks after his father had died. Then, less than a year later, how she'd taken off with a "boyfriend," leaving Cole and his brother behind.

Meg had seen Cole's stepdad only once, coming out of a downtown bar at two in the afternoon, drunk.

"Of course—" Meg chose her words carefully, wanting to be fair "—if you'd like us to consider other parenting styles, I'm certainly open to the possibility."

Cole waved a dismissive hand. "Making joint decisions and presenting a united front works for me."

"It's all about *communication*." She stressed the last

word, remembering how he'd dropped her so abruptly and refused her calls.

"So." He picked up a shiny purple eggplant, stared at it for a moment with a puzzled look on his face before putting it down. "What do you want to do about the party?"

Meg added some bananas, oranges and a pineapple to the growing mound of food. "On one hand, I think it'd be fun for Charlie to play with my nephews. And we'd know some of the people there. The food is bound to be fabulous. Travis raves about Lexi's cooking."

"On the other hand…" Cole prompted, adding a gallon of milk and a carton of orange juice to the basket.

"Charlie just lost his parents. Is being tossed into such a busy environment really what he needs right now?" Meg sighed. She'd often thought the world would be a better place if children came with instruction booklets.

"Well, he has some upcoming days off school. That will give him lots of one-on-one time with us." Cole's brows pulled together in thought. "Having children to play with might be a nice break for him."

Cole made a good point. Meg had never considered it from that perspective before. Now, she recalled how excited Charlie had been about attending this birthday party. Playing with kids his own age had been a big part of his life prior to his parents' deaths. The boy probably did miss the interaction.

"I could call Lexi when we get back to the house and tell her we accept their offer," Meg said. "Or I suppose I can just wait and tell her at church tomorrow."

"Church?" Cole couldn't have looked more shocked if she'd said they were going to an orgy. "I didn't say anything about church."

"I don't know about you, but church is a part of my life," Meg said with a smile. "And I know Charlie is looking forward to going to Sunday school tomorrow. I thought we'd go to church, then while he's at Sunday school have breakfast at The Coffee Pot. According to my brother, the café is still 'the' place to go on Sunday mornings.".

Meg hadn't been surprised to hear that the small café had retained its well-deserved reputation as having the best breakfast menu in Jackson.

"I guess it's better than sitting at home staring at four walls." Cole maneuvered the cart down the canned vegetable aisle with surprising agility. "That's when I start thinking about Ty and Joy and the unfairness of it all."

A lump formed in Meg's throat. "Last night I dreamed I saw them in this supermarket. They were laughing and talking with each other when I saw them. I was so happy. But each time I tried to approach them, they kept disappearing down another aisle. For some reason they couldn't hear me, not even when I called out to them. I woke up crying."

Tears welled in Meg's eyes but she brushed them back and threw a couple cans into the cart.

Before she could take off down the aisle, Cole reached over and briefly squeezed her hand. "I'm going to make an executive decision."

Meg blinked. "I don't understand."

He confiscated two cans of spinach from the cart and placed them back on the shelf. "We don't need these."

Meg could feel the heat flooding her cheeks. "I can't believe I did that."

"Grief makes us do all sorts of crazy things." Cole shot her an understanding smile.

"I miss her, them, so much," Meg said with a sigh. "But I'm still thankful."

Cole maneuvered the cart to the side to let an attractive brunette go past. He didn't appear to notice the woman's appraising look and the increased sway of her hips as she sauntered past him. "Thankful for what?"

Her heart cried at the trace of bitterness in his tone.

"Thankful that Joy and Ty were responsible parents who took time to update their will and name us as guardians for their son." Meg lifted a can of peas from the shelf. When Cole nodded, she dropped the can into the cart. "If they hadn't, Charlie would have been thrust into the foster care system until the courts had time to decide where he should be placed."

A shocked look blanketed Cole's face. "Seriously?"

Meg nodded. "And I'm thankful that Charlie walked away from the crash without a scratch. I saw pictures of the car." She shuddered. "It's a miracle anyone made it out of the vehicle alive."

Cole looked at Meg as if seeing her for the first time.

"Not to mention the improbability of you and I making living together under the same roof work…yet we're doing it." She tossed another couple cans into the cart. As far as she was concerned, having them peacefully—at least so far—coexist under the same roof was a miracle.

"You've convinced me." He released his hold on the cart and lifted both hands in a gesture of surrender. "We do have a lot to be thankful for."

He reached into the cart and pulled out a can. "But seriously, creamed corn?"

Meg confiscated the can from his hand and put it back in the cart. "I happen to love the stuff. If you and Charlie don't, so sad for you. It'll just mean more for me."

Chapter Seven

When Cole's dad had been alive, they'd attended Sunday services as a family every week. Once he died, everything changed.

If Cole said he missed being at church, he'd be lying. He hadn't had any use for the place since God had taken the only good thing in his life. His dad had understood Cole's struggles in school, had supported his pursuit of excellence on the football field. Most of all, his father had loved him unconditionally.

Cole's mother had seemed more relieved than saddened by her husband's death from cancer. She'd remarried before the man she'd vowed to love forever was even cold in the ground.

"My mommy said when I make a mean face, it could freeze like that."

Cole pulled his thoughts back to the present and turned

in his seat to face his son sitting in the back. "Was I scowling?"

The child pulled his brows together, narrowed his eyes then pointed to his own face.

"Wow," Cole said. "If my face froze like that, I'd scare you *and* Aunt Meg."

Though her eyes remained focused on the road, Meg chuckled. "After that movie last night, I don't think I can stand one more scary thing."

Cole and Charlie exchanged smiles. Meg had closed her eyes when the hunter came after Bambi's mother. Though Cole would never admit it, he'd found himself hoping Bambi's mother had gotten away.

"I liked the movie," Cole said. "Did you like it, Charlie?"

The child had been mostly silent on the car ride into Jackson. "I liked it okay."

"Is something on your mind, honey?" Meg voiced the question Cole wasn't sure he should ask.

He knew the boy had been traumatized. While Cole wanted Charlie to know he cared, he didn't want to force the child to talk about his feelings before he was ready.

"I dunno." Charlie kicked his foot against the back of the seat.

Cole waited, a thousand questions on the tip of his tongue. Most of the articles he'd read on grief in kids said not to press, to be patient. The trouble was, he'd never been a particularly patient person.

"What's an orphan?" Charlie asked, just as Meg pulled into the church parking lot. "At the funeral Tommy Grosscup said I was an orphan, like that was something bad."

Cole's heart sank. He glanced at Meg. While he'd learned a great deal reading all those articles, she'd had real-life experience raising her siblings.

"An orphan," Meg said softly, "is someone who doesn't have any parents. I'm an orphan because I lost both my mom and dad. Uncle Cole isn't an orphan because his mother is still living."

"So I was an orphan," Charlie said, "but I'm not any-more."

Once again, Cole forced his mouth to remain shut. Meg simply smiled, projecting an air of calm acceptance that Cole envied.

"That's right," she said after a long moment. "You're not an orphan because—"

"I have you and Uncle Cole for my mommy and daddy," Charlie said as if the answer was obvious.

A tightness filled Cole's chest and he saw Meg blink back tears.

Ryan had been right. Charlie needed a father *and* a mother during this difficult time.

Though Meg wouldn't be around forever, for the first time Cole was grateful she was here now. And once she was gone Cole would start seriously looking for a woman who'd be a wife to him and a mother to his son.

A friend. A lover. Most important, a woman he could trust.

Meg slowed her steps as she and Cole approached the front door of The Coffee Pot. "Travis said they usually commandeer a big table at the back of the place."

Cole had run into Meg's brother several times when he'd been in Jackson Hole visiting Joy and Ty. He knew Travis from high school football and they'd always gotten along. But in the ensuing years, whenever he'd spoken with the young doctor, there had been a decided coolness to their interaction.

While Cole had never mentioned his relationship with

Meg to any of the guys on the football team—and he'd kept their breakup to himself, as well—he had the feeling Meg had given her brother an earful. And a one-sided earful if Travis's response was any indication.

Suddenly, the thought of breakfast with *her* relatives and *her* friends held little appeal.

"Why don't you go in, spend time with your brother." Cole glanced down the almost-deserted sidewalk. Because of the brisk north wind, once people got out of their vehicles, they didn't loiter but headed straight inside. "I'm going to take a little walk."

"Get real, macho man." Meg grabbed his arm and pulled him toward the door. "It's too cold to take a walk. Not to mention the sidewalk has a glaze of ice an inch thick on top of it. If you don't feel like talking, just sit there and eat."

Meg wasn't sure what was behind Cole's reticence and she didn't care. If he felt awkward, too bad. She'd felt awkward in church, strolling down the aisle with him. She was going to feel even more awkward walking into the café holding his arm, like she was his girlfriend. In fact, she suddenly found herself wishing she didn't have to go inside.

But life was about pushing past the hard times, so Meg walked through the door, releasing Cole's arm the instant they crossed the threshold.

As she'd expected, the place buzzed with wall-to-wall people. Travis stood and waved to her from the back of the café. The table was full, other than the two seats he'd saved next to him.

Cole appeared surprised by the warm welcome he received, but easily fell into the conversation. With him looking so relaxed, Meg doubted anyone at the table had a clue that he'd had second thoughts about joining them.

Once the waitress had taken their orders and poured

her a cup of coffee, the tension in Meg's shoulders began to ease.

She sipped the strong cowboy blend and let her gaze linger on her brother, who was doing his best to draw Cole out and make him feel welcome. Apparently Travis had bought the explanation she'd given him regarding her relationship with Cole.

Though Meg normally could hold her own in any conversation, instead of talking, she listened and found herself learning more about Cole. She told herself since they were sharing custody it was important for her to know as much about him as possible.

"I can't believe you got out of college and immediately started a business," Lexi said in an admiring tone. "How does that happen?"

"Lots of luck and not knowing any better." Cole chuckled. "I earned a degree in entrepreneurship at the University of Texas, so I thought starting a business was what you were supposed to do once you had that diploma in hand."

Nick leaned forward, resting his forearms on the table, his intelligent eyes bright with interest. "What did you use for start-up cash?"

"My uncle lent me some money, which I paid back within the first two years."

Meg heard the pride in Cole's voice. To have come so far was an amazing accomplishment, especially considering the type of home life he'd had.

"How many franchises do you have now?" Travis asked. Even though her brother had appeared to be engrossed in a side conversation with David Wahl, his lifelong friend and brother-in-law, he'd obviously been paying attention.

"Forty franchises in seven states." Cole took a sip of coffee. "If everything comes together the way it should, Jackson Hole will be number forty-one."

"You're going to open one here?" Meg didn't know why she was so surprised. The economy in Jackson was booming and cowboys and skiers loved their coffee.

"Your omelet, sir."

"Looking that way," Cole answered, flashing the waitress a smile that had been winning him hearts since grade school.

When the college-age girl batted her long lashes in response, Meg stomped firmly down on an unwelcome surge of jealousy. Why should it matter to her who Cole flirted with? He could give the woman his phone number for all she cared. Except, of course, that such an action would send Charlie a bad message.

But just like at the grocery store, the fact that the waitress was pretty and definitely interested didn't seem to matter to him. He merely added some Tabasco to his eggs and returned to the conversation.

"I'm looking at the possibility of living part of the year in Austin, where my corporate offices are located, and part of the year in Jackson Hole." His gaze turned to Derek Rossi, a former professional baseball player, seated to his right. "I understand that, like Nick and Lexi, you and your wife don't live here year-round. How is that working for you?"

"It's difficult," Derek admitted. As an expert sports commentator for a major network, Derek spent much of the baseball season on the road. "Rachel and I would prefer to just live here. That's not a possibility at this time. The hardest part is working around Mickie's school schedule."

"That's the same struggle we face with Addie," Nick chimed in. "Thankfully our girl is very social. She has friends in Dallas as well as friends here."

"Even so, we know it'd be easier on her to be in one

home or the other," Lexi added, and Rachel, Derek's pretty blonde wife, nodded her agreement.

Cole took a bite of his omelet and chewed, a thoughtful look on his face. "According to the provisions of the will, I need to stay in Jackson Hole at least through the school year. Because of that, I'm planning on delegating a few more functions to my management team. Loosening that control will be a good first step if I decide to move here permanently."

"Thankfully, with the internet, you can stay connected wherever you live," Nick said. "But I can tell you right now you're going to miss those football Saturdays in Austin. There's nothing here that compares to that game-day atmosphere."

The conversation shifted to college football, a subject on which all the guys at the table seemed to have an opinion.

Meg picked at her waffle, unable to shake a feeling of unease. It wasn't until the waitress brought the check that she realized what was troubling her.

Cole had spoken of his future plans as if he was Charlie's sole guardian. He hadn't mentioned her involvement at all. It was as if she didn't exist, or matter.

What arrogance, to not even consider her feelings or her plans. To simply assume she would go along with whatever *he* decided was best.

Earlier, Meg would have asserted that she and Cole had made great strides in their working relationship over the past few days and were on the same page regarding Charlie's welfare.

Now it seemed that in the course of one meal, they'd somehow taken a giant leap backward.

By the time they picked up Charlie from Sunday school, the snow that had laid down an additional blanket of white overnight had resumed falling. Worse yet, the wind had picked up, whipping the flakes against the windshield and limiting visibility.

Cole released the breath he'd been holding when Meg finally pulled into the garage. He took a second to massage his quads before unfastening his seat belt and stepping out of the vehicle. Though he didn't feel he needed the crutches anymore, he was beginning to realize how much stress they'd taken off his leg. And how much the cold made his leg ache.

Since Charlie hadn't gone to breakfast with them, once inside Meg heated up some soup and made the boy a sandwich. Afterward, she surprised Cole by asking him to read to him while she cleaned up the kitchen.

Cole had to admit that when Meg shoved a stack of books at him, for a second a panic rose inside him. In that instant he was back in school. Making a joke when a teacher asked him to read aloud. Struggling to understand test instructions. And always, though he never showed it, feeling stupid.

He glanced at the books in his hand. Knowing his history, why had she asked him to read?

Still, it was okay. Thanks to his uncle, after all those years of not understanding the reason for his difficulty reading, he'd finally gotten a diagnosis—dyslexia—and the help he'd needed. Instead of barely getting by, like he had in high school, he'd graduated from college with honors. Along the way he'd tried to make up for all he'd missed.

That's why it was important to him that Charlie love books and become a good reader.

"Which one should we look at first?" Cole spread the books out on the coffee table, amazed at all the bright covers and quirky titles. "I don't know how you're going to choose. They all look good."

Charlie studied them for several seconds then pointed at a yellow book with a monkey on the cover. "That one."

"Curious George's ABCs." Cole read the title as he picked it up.

"My teacher read it to us in class." Charlie's voice reverberated with eagerness. "Curious George is always getting into trouble. He's a funny monkey."

"I bet he is," Cole said, smiling.

"You never read it?" Charlie scrambled to sit beside Cole on the sofa. "My teacher said he'd read all the Curious George books by the time he was our age."

Cole thought for a moment, contemplating how to explain to his son that he hadn't read a book for pleasure until he was in college. "I didn't read much as a kid—"

"I don't, either," Charlie said immediately. "I don't like books."

"I love them," Cole responded. The last thing he wanted was to turn Charlie against reading. "Where else but in books can you spend time with a pirate? Or a ninja? Or a funny monkey learning his ABCs?"

Charlie's gaze narrowed. "I thought you said you didn't read books."

"My dad had difficulty reading and he didn't like books in the house." Cole hesitated. Should he tell Charlie that he'd also had trouble with his letters? Or was that too much information for a small boy to process?

He was still debating in his head how much to divulge, when Charlie spoke.

"We're learning our ABCs now and it's hard." A shadow briefly passed across the child's face. "My teacher says it will get easier."

"It will." Cole offered the boy an encouraging smile.

While it hadn't gotten better for his dad, back then no one knew what dyslexia was, much less how to work around it. When Cole had been a boy, it hadn't been much better.

Banishing the unpleasant memories, Cole picked up the book and flipped it open to the first page, then glanced at Charlie. "Shall we see what Curious George is doing?"

Charlie snuggled up against him. "Yeah."

"Are you cold?"

"Nope." Charlie rested his cheek against Cole's arm. "Uncle Cole."

"Yes, Charlie?"

"You're not going to leave me, are you?"

Cole's heart twisted. Until now he hadn't realized the depths of the little boy's fears. "Nope. You're stuck with me, buckaroo. I'm not going anywhere."

"What about Aunt Meg?"

With those blue eyes—so like his own—focused on him and shining with blind trust, Cole hesitated, not sure how to answer. While he didn't want to lie—

"I'm not going anywhere, either, honey."

At the sound of the feminine voice, Cole turned. Meg stood in the doorway to the kitchen, still wearing the brown wraparound dress she'd worn to church. She wiped her hands on a red-and-white-checkered dish towel, the picture of domestic bliss.

"Of course, Uncle Cole and I probably won't always live in the same house," she added.

Cole knew there was no *probably* about it.

Charlie's brows pulled together in distress. "Are you going to get a divorce?"

Crossing the room, Meg took a seat in the chair opposite the sofa, her eyes looking more green than hazel in the light.

"Do you really want to get into this now?" Cole murmured, his tone making it clear he preferred to wait.

"Yes," she said in a soft but firm tone. "Yes, I do."

Her gaze locked with his before she turned her attention to the boy, who was now sitting up straight as a soldier on the sofa.

"Charlie." Meg leaned forward, resting her forearms on her thighs, her smile open and friendly. "Do you know what it means when a couple gets a divorce?"

"Dana Murray's parents got divorced. They don't live together anymore," Charlie said, clearly warming to the topic. "Dana's dad has a girlfriend and her mom is really mad. She hates him. Dana hates him, too."

"I'm sure she doesn't hate him." Cole felt a pang of sympathy for Dana's father, a man he didn't even know. He couldn't imagine how he'd feel if Charlie hated *him*.

"Yes, she does," Charlie said. "She—"

"What's happening between Dana's parents has nothing to do with how they feel about her," Meg said. "What's between her mom and dad is grown-up stuff. I'm sure it makes her sad that her daddy doesn't live with them anymore. But that doesn't mean she and her daddy can't enjoy spending time together."

"But her daddy didn't even come to conferences," Charlie said.

Cole raised a brow. "Conferences?"

"I assume Charlie is talking about the parent-teacher conferences they have at school."

"My mommy *and* daddy came." Charlie nodded his head up and down. "Afterward, we all went out for ice cream."

"Well, even when Uncle Cole and I don't live together," Meg said, "we'll still come to your conferences together."

She glanced at him for confirmation and Cole reluctantly nodded.

Tears filled Charlie's eyes and his gaze sought Cole's. "Don't live together? You *are* getting a divorce from Aunt Meg."

The words came out on a wail. If the boy wasn't so distressed, Cole might have felt the urge to laugh. To get divorced implied you first had gotten married. He and Meg? Not a chance in hell.

"We're not getting a divorce, buddy." Cole gentled his tone and took his son's hand in his. "Aunt Meg and I are just friends."

The statement was a stretch, but desperate times called for desperate measures.

"We're only living in the same house now because I need help with my knee," Cole continued. "And because Aunt Meg hadn't found a place of her own yet."

"That's right," Meg said. "Hopefully once Uncle Cole is better, I'll be able to find a little apartment not far away."

Charlie wiped his runny nose against his shirtsleeve, tears clinging to the tips of his lashes.

"You'll have a bedroom at your uncle Cole's place and one at mine." Meg's smile appeared forced. "Two bedrooms of your very own. Won't that be fun?"

Charlie's jaw set in a stubborn tilt and he whipped his head from side to side. "I like it here. I want all of us to live here together."

The boy's eyes might be filled with fire, but the trembling of his bottom lip gave him away. Cole realized that in their desire to be honest with the child, they'd caused him needless worry.

After all, Charlie wouldn't be shuttled back and forth between two houses; he'd be with him. With his father. But too much had already been said on the topic. Changing the subject seemed wise.

"I like it here, too." Cole spoke in a hearty tone, hoping Meg would pick up on it and play along. "My bed is so comfortable that it's difficult for me to get up in the morning. In fact, right now I'm thinking about sinking into that soft mattress and taking a nap."

"Naps are for babies," Charlie asserted, though Cole could see the lines of fatigue around the boy's eyes.

"No one ever told me that," Meg said. "I take naps all the time."

Cole pretended to yawn. "I think I'm going to stretch out on that big bed of mine and rest my eyes."

"Maybe we could all rest our eyes for a few minutes?" Meg said.

"I'm all for it." Cole forced an extra-hearty tone.

"I've an idea." Charlie bounced up and down on the sofa. "We'll all take a nap together on Uncle Cole's bed. Doesn't that sound like fun?"

Out of the corner of his eye, Cole caught the look of startled surprise that skittered across Meg's face. Because the light had returned to Charlie's eyes, Cole shoved aside his own misgivings and grinned. "Great idea, son. What do you say, Meg? Care to join me in bed?"

Chapter Eight

Meg kept her arms firmly plastered to her side and tried to tell herself that lying on top of Cole Lassiter's bed was no big deal.

After all, Charlie was between them and she had on all her clothes. Not to mention the California king went on forever. You could easily have five people on it and they'd never touch. Which was good because *touching* Cole was the last thing on Meg's mind this afternoon.

She'd heard the challenge in his voice when he'd asked if she wanted to join him in bed. He'd been taunting her. Confident she'd turn him down. Which she wouldn't have had trouble doing if it hadn't been for Charlie and the pleading look in his eyes.

Talking about her and Cole going their separate ways and sharing custody had been an error in judgment. Charlie had lost his parents only weeks ago. To even mention more change to the boy at this time didn't make any sense.

Cole realized it, too. She knew that's why he'd started talking about naps. And why the three of them were now lying on his bed with the shades drawn.

Meg closed her eyes. She'd almost drifted off to sleep when Cole murmured something to her, something she couldn't quite hear. Hoping he didn't expect to have a conversation with Charlie already asleep between them, Meg pushed herself up on one elbow.

She breathed a sigh of relief when she saw that his eyes were shut and his lips now silent. She hadn't realized that he talked in his sleep. Of course, that was understandable considering they'd never spent the night together.

Even when they'd been sneaking around seeing each other, she hadn't known all that much about him. Oh, she'd known that he loved animals and had a sense of humor in sync with her own. She knew he had a lot of friends and rarely said an unkind word about anyone. He'd even befriended Chip before championing the underdog was cool. Still, what made him tick had remained a mystery.

Other than the time he'd confided that he had difficulty reading, he'd shared very little personal information. The fact that he'd graduated from college and started his own successful business made her wonder if the confession had been merely a ploy to make her think he was sharing something of importance with her.

She'd believed him. Had worried about his reading difficulties. And, though Cole had sworn her to silence, she'd even sought the advice of her father—an English teacher at the local high school—on how to help someone who'd reached seventeen without being able to read well. Her father had asked who this person was, but all she'd told him was "a friend," not wanting to betray Cole's confidence.

It hadn't mattered. Within days of his confession, in fact the day after he'd taken her innocence in the backseat of that old Chevy, he quit calling. When she saw him in school he walked by as if she didn't exist.

Being young and foolish and convinced she was in love, she'd waited a couple of days before tossing aside her pride and calling him. She'd realized it was over when he didn't call her back. Then her folks had died.

Her world had suddenly been turned upside down. She'd desperately needed someone to hold her close and tell her she would survive…and she'd still hoped that person would be Cole. But he hadn't shown his face at either the visitation or the funeral. Considering all they'd shared, his absence had been a slap in the face.

She collapsed back against the pillow and closed her eyes, letting sleep steal her away from the memories she wished she could forget….

Meg told herself to wake up, but the dream was so compelling she couldn't leave it, not yet. Cole had come to her.

With a contented sigh, she wrapped her arms around his broad shoulders. Her head fit perfectly against his chest, just under his chin. Having him so close was a dream come true.

She loved the way he smelled, a woodsy mixture of cologne and soap and maleness that brought a tingle to her lips and heat percolating low in her belly.

His hand flattened against her lower back, drawing her up against the length of his body. Meg pressed herself more fully against him, the action bringing back memories of when they'd made love.

The man now holding her in his arms had been the first to kiss her, to touch her, to make love to her. But once wasn't enough.

She longed to once again run her hands over his body, to feel the coiled strength of skin and muscle sliding under her fingers. She wanted him to touch her in the same way, wanted to feel the weight of his body on hers. Wanted to feel him inside her.

She planted a kiss at the base of his neck, his skin salty beneath her lips.

"Are you sure this is wise?" The words seemed to come from far away.

Of all the times for her conscience to make an appearance. Even in a dream, participating in a fantasy wasn't always wise. But she couldn't stop. Didn't *want* to stop. Being in Cole's arms felt so right.

She wound her arms around his neck and lifted her face.

He folded her more fully into his arms, anchoring her against his chest as his mouth covered hers in a deep, compelling kiss. Dreamily, Meg stroked his thick hair. He tasted as sweet as spearmint candy from The Coffee Pot.

His hand closed over one breast, cupping it high in his hand, circling the peak with his fingers. Meg inhaled sharply and, for a second, panicked. Until she remembered that this was a dream and there was no reason to deny herself anything.

If he'd noticed her momentary hesitation, he gave no indication. He continued to kiss her with a slow thoroughness that left her weak, trembling and longing for more. When his tongue swept across her lips, seeking access, she eagerly opened her mouth to him, pulling his body on top of hers, her tongue fencing with his.

The warmth in her lower belly turned fiery hot and became a pulsating need. There was only one problem. There were clothes between them. Thankfully she had a solution....

She slipped her hand between them, smiling when she encountered a hard bulge, closing her fingers over the strained zipper, anticipation coursing up her spine.

"Aunt Meg?"

Her fingers stilled. Was that Charlie's voice? What was the child doing in her R-rated—soon to be X-rated—dream? A moment later she heard his voice again, more insistent this time.

Though every fiber of her being longed to ride this dream through to completion, Meg reluctantly opened her eyes…and found herself face-to-face with Cole Lassiter.

Cole knew he should have pushed Meg away when she'd first snuggled up against him. But they were alone—Charlie had long since gotten up and headed into the living room to watch cartoons—and she'd looked so beautiful lying there, that he couldn't resist. He'd wrapped his arm around her, his heart experiencing a tug of déjà vu in the process.

When she kissed his neck, he somehow found the words to ask if she was *sure*. Sure she knew what she was doing. Sure this was really a road she wanted to go down. Her answer had been to twine her hands around his neck and lift her lips to his.

From the shock in her eyes now, she obviously was having some second thoughts about that decision.

Cole rolled off of her, sensing by the murderous look on her face that being tossed to the floor was a distinct possibility. Only when he was flat on his back did he realize they weren't alone. Charlie stood at the foot of the bed.

"My daddy used to kiss my mommy like that," the boy said in a pleased tone. Charlie cocked his head and rocked back on the heels of his cowboy boots. "Can I have a soda?"

"Sure." Meg's voice sounded strangled. "Just make sure not to spill."

"'Kay." The boy tossed the word over his shoulder as he raced from the room.

Charlie had barely disappeared from sight when Meg punched Cole in the shoulder.

"What did you think you were doing?" she sputtered. "Kissing me like that?"

"You started it." Cole pushed himself to a sitting position, his jeans tight enough to strangle, his heart pounding an irregular rhythm. His head may have gotten the message the fun was over, but his body definitely hadn't.

"What do you mean *I* started it?" She sat up, her hair a tangled mass of auburn curls.

"Charlie left to watch cartoons. I was lying here, minding my own business, trying to decide if I should get up, when you kissed my neck." Even as his body responded to her touch, he'd told himself to push her away.

But then he'd taken a deep breath and his good intentions had been lost. Her perfume, a light floral fragrance, reminded him of spring. And of the good times they'd once shared.

"I was sleeping," Meg asserted, color high in her cheeks. "I didn't know what I was doing."

He snorted. Granted, she'd kept her eyes closed, but she'd been awake enough to respond to his question.

"I *asked* if you thought this was wise," he said, meeting her gaze head-on. "You responded by kissing me."

She opened her mouth then shut it. After a long moment her lips turned up in a rueful smile. "Okay, I admit it. I was a willing participant in the madness."

"You were?" His voice rose.

"I thought I was dreaming." She pushed her hair back from her face with one hand. "But that doesn't change the fact that I wanted to kiss you. If Charlie hadn't come in, I probably would have gone a lot further."

For a second he wondered if she was playing with him. Until he remembered her fingers on his zipper. His body stirred in response. "Seriously?"

The pink in her cheeks deepened and she shrugged. "What can I say? It's that same crazy physical attraction that brought us together way back when."

Cole pushed on his bad leg—hard—and the sharp stab of pain told him he wasn't dreaming. But he had to be. It made no sense that Meg would confess her, well, her *lust* for him.

"You feel it, too. Don't bother to deny it." Meg's gaze dropped to just below his belt buckle. "I'm a medical professional. I recognize the signs."

His maleness surged as her gaze lingered.

"I have no intention of denying it," he said in a gravelly voice.

From the moment she'd shown up on his radar screen, he'd wanted her with an intensity he couldn't explain. She'd been standing by her locker in the old high school, baggy gold sweater, modest plaid skirt showing off long shapely legs, auburn curls spilling down her back.

Jackson Hole High wasn't that big of a school. Even though he and Margaret didn't run in the same social circle, he'd known she was Travis Fisher's sister, the oldest girl in a family of eight. President of the science club. Honor Society member. And, unlike most of her female classmates, a girl who appeared to prefer the brainy geeks in her accelerated classes to football stars.

Usually when he saw her, she had guys like Ed Rice, class valedictorian, hanging around. But this time she'd been alone.

"Large breasts." Meg pointed a thumb to her chest. "That's why you liked me."

Her words brought Cole back to the present with a jolt.

He could tell her there had been lots of girls back then with big boobs, er, breasts. She'd been different. But what would be the point?

"There's nothing wrong with physical attraction," he said. "That's the only reason you agreed to take that walk with me."

Even as the words left his lips, he hesitated. Meg hadn't been a football groupie. If she was, she'd have talked about things that interested him, instead of English literature.

The second they'd begun strolling through the Elk Refuge, she'd launched into a discussion of the books they'd read in class. Or rather, ones he should have read. Any knowledge he had of the novels had been based entirely on tidbits gleaned from class discussion. Or the movie version he'd rented from the video store.

She'd obviously been nervous, searching for common ground. Yet all her chatter did was to emphasize the differences between them. Surprisingly the attraction remained.

"I wanted to kiss you," she admitted.

"The physical pull was strong."

"Though I liked the kissing," she said slowly as if choosing her words carefully, "I thought our relationship went beyond the physical."

He'd thought there was more to it, too. When he told her he loved her, he'd meant it.

Cole wasn't quite sure why she was acting as if she'd cared for him back then. Thanks to her good friend Ed Rice, he knew what she'd really thought of him. Intellectually, Cole had been judged and found wanting.

"I had no complaints with the sex," he said, swinging his legs to the side of the bed.

What puzzled him most was how he could still desire someone who had no respect for him.

"Why did you quit calling? Was there another girl? You

could have simply told me if there was someone else. I know all the girls liked you."

Uh-oh. Cole recognized the rapid speech and run-together sentences. Though Meg wasn't normally a big talker, the floodgates had been opened and he was going to get an earful.

"Even Joy." Meg gave a humorless laugh at his startled look. "Yep, my best friend had it bad for you. She never admitted it, at least not to me, but I could tell."

Joy. She was bringing up Joy? And here he'd thought the conversation couldn't get any worse.

"Travis suspected that you and I had been involved." Meg picked at a piece of lint from her shirt. "But I never told him I slept with you."

Thank God for small favors. Her older brother had never been a violent guy, but all the boys knew that nobody messed with the Fisher girls.

"Travis was surprised you didn't come to our parents' funeral, seeing as how you'd played ball together all those years," Meg continued. "You were the only one on the team not there."

It would be so easy to dismiss those feelings, but Cole remembered how he'd felt when his friends had shown up for his dad's funeral.

"Sorry about that." He bent over and tightened a strap on his brace. "Something came up."

"What could have been so important, Cole?" She spat his name as if it tasted bitter on her tongue. "So important that you couldn't have shown my family—and me—a little respect?"

The car accident that had claimed the lives of her parents had occurred in late spring. One more year. That's all Cole had to make it through before he would graduate.

Then he'd take his brother and get the hell out of Jackson Hole.

The wrong person seeing that black eye could have ruined those plans. If they'd gone into foster care, all bets would have been off.

Cole jumped to his feet, stifling a curse when his knee revolted at the sudden movement. He gritted his teeth and rounded the bed to where she stood, her arms tightly crossed and clasped to her chest.

After what she'd done, she didn't deserve an explanation from him. Well, she was going to get one anyway.

"Do you want to know why I didn't come to the funeral?"

"It doesn't matter now," she muttered with a dismissive wave. "That was a long time ago."

Her words said one thing, but the ramrod straightness of her back and the tight set to her shoulders told him it did matter.

Perhaps another man would have held back the truth. Some might even say he'd be justified after what she'd done to him. But in his mind two wrongs never equaled a right.

"I had a black eye," he said. "I knew it'd raise questions if I came to the funeral with the side of my face looking like it'd been run through a meat grinder."

Surprise mixed with puzzlement in her gaze. "How were you injured?"

"My stepdad used me for a punching bag," he said in the same tone he might use to describe what he'd had for supper. He ignored the shock skittering across Meg's face and continued. "It only happened when he drank. Unfortunately that was pretty much all the time."

"Oh, Cole." Meg gasped, bringing two fingers to her lips. "I never knew."

"A couple of teachers suspected. I denied it." He turned and walked to the window, gazing unseeingly out over the pine trees blanketed with snow.

"Why didn't you tell them the truth? They could have—"

"What could they have done?" He turned and faced her, his back against the windowsill. It seemed oddly symbolic since he'd felt as if his back had been against the wall from the moment his mother had left him and his brother behind. "They'd have turned Cade and me over to social services. We'd likely have been split up. Putting up with Wally was better than taking that chance."

"Maybe they could have found a way to keep you and your brother together—"

"Yeah, and maybe Santa Claus is real." He raked a hand through his hair and expelled a harsh breath. "I couldn't take the chance."

Her brows pulled together. "It sounds like this went on for quite some time. I can't understand how none of the teachers noticed the abuse."

"Wally made sure he hit me where the bruises didn't show." A chill settled over Cole's body. "I started football in middle school and played hard. That explained away any bruises. By the time I met you I could hold my own against him."

"What about Cade?"

"For some reason he left him alone." Cole gave a humorless laugh. "Other than the night I got the black eye. I stepped between them. There was no way I was going to let him pound on my little brother. After that episode Wally gave both of us a wide berth. Once I graduated from high school, I left Jackson and took Cade with me."

Contacting an uncle in Austin who he'd never met had

been a long shot, but it had worked out. Cole only wished he'd done it years before.

Soft fingers touched his arm and he jerked his gaze upward to find Meg standing beside him.

"Why didn't you tell *me* about your stepdad?"

"Like I said, I told no one." He met her gaze. "It was best."

"I'd have been there for you."

Cole gazed down into her luminous green eyes and realized how easy it would be to fall under her spell once again. To believe in the words sliding so easily from her soft lips. To think she genuinely cared and could be trusted.

But he wouldn't let himself be fooled a second time. Meg was a nice person with many good qualities.

Yet, trust her?

Not again. Not ever again.

Chapter Nine

The next week passed uneventfully for Meg. Life in her temporary mountain home settled into an easy rhythm. She helped Cole with his exercises and was astounded by his progress. Her only worry was Charlie. The boy had begun to suck his thumb and had started waking up during the night crying.

Yesterday, he'd had his first session with Dr. Allman, a Jackson psychologist who came highly recommended by July Wahl. Charlie appeared to enjoy his time with the man, saying Dr. Pete had a lot of really cool toys.

Maybe everything with Charlie was under control. *Her and Cole?* Well, that relationship was still under construction.

When Cole had opened up to her Sunday afternoon about his childhood abuse, she felt as if something momentous had occurred. She now understood him in a way she never had before. His honesty had chipped away at the hurt and anger encasing her heart all these years.

Although Cole may not have explained why he'd so un-ceremoniously dumped her back then, now there were lots of potential explanations. Whatever the correct answer, Meg bet it had something to do with his tumultuous home life.

She considered asking him straight out, but he appeared more withdrawn after his confession, as if dredging up the past had shot a hole in his emotions.

"What's taking so long?"

Speak of the devil.

Meg glanced up from the kitchen counter, where she'd been preparing vegetables for Lexi's holiday festivities tomorrow, to find Cole standing in the doorway. For a second, she let her gaze linger, her eyes drinking him in. She'd never known a man who could look so good in jeans and a sweatshirt. She barely noticed the brace on his leg anymore. It had become as much a part of him as his dark hair and the barely perceptible cleft in his chin.

"Charlie sent me to tell you that we've got the Chutes and Ladders game out. All we're missing is you."

"Did he really say that?" Meg teased. "Or are you sim-ply hoping for some adult conversation with your pop-corn?"

While she was working on the veggies, Cole had stuck a bag of popcorn in the microwave. Charlie had done his part by dumping the finished product into a large bowl and carrying it into the family room.

"I'll have you know, Charlie and I were in the middle of a very scintillating conversation on the merits of chewing two pieces of gum over just one." Cole crossed the room and grabbed a couple of black olives from the relish tray in front of her. Before he'd finished chewing those, he reached for another.

"Stop that." She slapped his hand. "These are for tomorrow."

While she watched, Cole had the audacity to snag another olive.

"I thought Lexi had the food covered?"

"She does, but I hate the thought of going to a holiday dinner empty-handed. My mother always said—" Meg heaved an exasperated breath when Cole filched a piece of stuffed celery from the tray.

She opened her mouth to give him the dressing-down he deserved, when a look of pure delight blanketed his face.

"Wow, this is good." He chewed thoughtfully for another second then lifted a brow. "Do I taste crab in this?"

Meg nodded. "Along with chive cream cheese, onion salt and a few other ingredients."

"My mom used that store-bought pimento stuffing which I liked. But this—" he lifted up the last bite of celery "—*this* is an epicurean delight."

"I'm glad you like it." A wave of pleasure washed over Meg. "Travis told me Lexi is into gourmet cooking, so I wanted to bring something extra special."

Cole grabbed another celery stalk, resisting her attempt to snatch it from his hand.

"Sure you don't want to leave the tray here for the three of us to enjoy?" he asked.

The three of us.

The phrase had such a nice ring. Of course, nice ring or not, the current arrangement was just temporary. Before long, Cole would be able to care for Charlie on his own. There would be no more nights of board games and popcorn. It would be just Cole and Charlie. Or her and Charlie. Not the three of them.

Though Meg tried to tell herself that getting her own place would be a good thing, at the moment she had no burning desire to leave.

"I recognize that smile," Cole said. "I know what you're thinking."

Dear God, she hoped not.

"Tell me, oh, wise one," Meg managed to shoot back.

He lifted a radish she'd carved into a rose and bit off a petal. "You're thinking we could keep the tray and bring a bottle of wine instead."

"You know me too well." She breathed a sigh of relief, popped the lid on the tray, then slid it into the refrigerator.

"That I do."

The slightly mocking edge to his voice was back. Was sarcasm Cole's way of keeping women at arm's length?

Had someone hurt him the way he'd once hurt her? Was that the reason for the "I don't trust you" vibe she'd been getting from him since that first meeting in Ryan's office?

Although they now lived under the same roof, Meg realized she had very little knowledge of Cole's personal life since he'd left Jackson Hole. In fact, for all she knew, he could have someone special waiting for him back in Texas.

Meg slammed the refrigerator door shut with extra force and whirled. Telling herself to play it cool, she sauntered across the kitchen and stopped in front of him. She lifted her chin. "Do you have a girlfriend?"

Way to play it cool, Meg.

His lips twitched. Apparently he found her blunt question amusing. "Does this curiosity have anything to do with your thwarted attempt to seduce me?"

"What?" Meg took a deep breath and lowered her voice. "For the record, *you* were doing the seducing, mister. And you still haven't answered my question."

"I'm not involved with anyone," he said in an annoyed tone. "If I was, I wouldn't have touched you."

Relief rushed through Meg.

He narrowed his gaze. "What about you? Do you have some doctor or lawyer waiting for you back in Omaha?"

"My last relationship ended over a year ago." Meg lifted one shoulder in a shrug. "We were engaged but I broke it off when I realized I didn't love him. Not enough."

"Joy mentioned a couple of months ago that you'd never married," he said, as if talking about her marital status with her best friend wasn't anything out of the ordinary. "Coming from that big family, I thought you'd have settled down and had a half-dozen kids by now."

"That was the dream," she said with a wistful sigh. "But I learned long ago that life doesn't always turn out like we plan. That's why being able to be a mother to Charlie is such a blessing. He'll probably end up being my only child."

Cole shifted from one foot to the other and grimaced. From the pained look that crossed his face, she guessed his knee was giving him trouble.

"You say you're not involved with anyone at the moment." Meg had her answer, so there was no need to go further. Except now he was back in her life and she was curious what he'd been up to all these years. Though Joy had obviously kept Cole up-to-date on his former classmates—including her—she hadn't mentioned anything about him to Meg. She couldn't imagine that Cole had made it to thirty-two without making a trip down the aisle. "Were you ever married?"

He shook his head.

"Ever come close?"

"Not really." He shrugged. "Relationships take time.

Since I got out of college, building up my business has been my priority."

"That's too bad," she murmured, thinking it wasn't bad at all. Just the thought of Cole with another woman made her stomach hurt. "Having a purpose and working hard is good. But there's more to life."

Uncorking the bottle of wine sitting on the counter, she poured them each a splash. When Cole lifted the glass, she clinked hers against his. "To a balanced life."

"Cheers." Cole's lips curved upward. He leaned close just as she began to speak.

"You know what they say…" Meg stopped when the intoxicating scent of his cologne hit her nostrils. She inhaled deeply.

Cole placed his glass on the granite countertop and stared, an odd look in his eyes. "Tell me," he said, his finger tracing the rim of his glass, though his gaze remained focused on her. "What do they say?"

Meg licked her suddenly dry lips. *Don't do it,* she told herself. *Take a step back.*

Instead, she leaned close and whispered in his ear, "All work and no play makes Cole a dull boy."

Instead of playful, her voice came out husky and sexy, which wasn't her intent. Not at all.

His eyes darkened. "Are you suggesting we have a fling?"

A fling? Meg resisted the urge to laugh hysterically, wondering if it had been her breast brushing against his arm or her sexy tone that had given him such a crazy idea. All she could say was the thought of sleeping with him was…intriguing.

Intriguing? No. *Crazy* was a much better word for what he proposed.

"Because if you are…" Cole trailed a finger up the side

of her neck, his mouth so close she could feel his breath against her cheek. "I'd be interested."

Her head jerked back. "You would?"

"You have to admit," he said in a low seductive tone that both thrilled and scared her to death, "the spark is still there."

The shivers coursing up and down her spine seemed to indicate that was a true statement.

"What about Charlie?" Meg asked, then cursed herself for acting as if she was considering his suggestion. Which she wasn't. Not at all.

"We'd be discreet." Cole brushed his lips against hers. "He wouldn't suspect a thing."

Meg focused on breathing in and out. Her whole body quivered. "What happens when I move to my own place?"

The words seemed to come from away, from someone else's lips, certainly not from her own.

"We'd reevaluate," he said. "For now, living together under the same roof makes it easy to…connect."

"It's a big decision…" Meg gave herself a mental shake. *Just say no.* She pulled her gaze from those brilliant blue eyes and decided forming a coherent thought might be easier if she put a little distance between them. She took a step back, stumbling over her feet.

Cole reached out a steadying hand, making no mention of her attempted hasty retreat. His lips lifted in an easy smile. "No rush. We don't have to decide anything now."

"Hey," a small voice called from the other room. "Are we playing this game or not?"

Cole grabbed his wineglass and took a quick sip. "Duty calls."

He made it all the way to the doorway before he stopped and glanced over his shoulder. "Aren't you coming?"

"Right behind you." Finally her voice came through for her. It held a cool confidence that made her want to cheer.

When he disappeared from sight, instead of rushing after him, Meg picked up her glass and stared down into the dark burgundy liquid, her mind buzzing with the possibilities. The words from a country song from several years ago played in her head, "I'm not talkin' about forever. I'm just talkin' about tonight."

Could she do it? Could she enter into a purely sexual relationship with a man she'd once loved?

No, she told herself firmly, no, she couldn't.

He'd broken her heart once. There was no way she was letting him get close enough to do it again.

Cole moved his playing piece forward and wondered how best to retract his offer.

He couldn't believe he'd suggested to Meg that they sleep together....

Who was he kidding? He *could* easily believe it. The moment he'd lifted that soft mound of flesh in his hand and teased the nipple to a hard point, he'd imagined what it would be like to make love to her again. And again. And again.

Ever since that night, whenever he hopped into bed, he imagined her lying beside him, hair spread out on the pillow, the sweet scent of her perfume filling his nostrils. The softness of the sheets reminded him of the feel of her skin against his fingertips. He swore the taste of her mouth still lingered on his lips.

Even when he finally fell into an exhausted slumber, she permeated his dreams. On the surface, entering into a physical affair with her might appear to not make sense. Yet, perhaps such a relationship was a necessary evil.

Yes, that's how he should think of it, as a necessary evil.

Not only was he finding it incredibly hard to be under the same roof with her and not touch, there was another reason a physical relationship with Meg should be given careful consideration.

This would be a way to get her out of his system once and for all. If he'd learned anything from his years of dating, it was that the hot-and-heavy phase never lasted.

With Meg, he'd broken it off before the sizzle had a chance to fizzle.

Necessary evil, he reminded himself.

Somehow the thought cheered him.

"Uncle Cole, you get to climb the ladder." Charlie's voice resonated with excitement.

Cole obligingly moved his piece to where his son indicated. He glanced up to find Meg staring and impulsively shot her a wink. "My reward for being a good boy."

She seemed confused by the comment, so he pointed to the good-deed square he'd landed on that showed him "sweeping up a mess."

Meg rolled her eyes. "Your turn, Charlie."

The child gave the arrow a spin.

"Uh-oh," Meg said.

Charlie stared at the game board. His smile faded.

"Looks like you pulled a cat's tail, my boy." Though he wanted to smile, Cole kept his expression serious. "It's down the chute for you."

To his shock and dismay, tears filled the boy's eyes. "I didn't mean to be bad."

Now Charlie's tears fell in earnest.

Sitting on the floor in front of the fire, Cole exchanged a glance with Meg. He wasn't sure what was going on. All he knew was it went beyond poor sportsmanship.

"Charlie." Meg opened her arms to the boy, who sat

cross-legged on the floor to her right. "Come over here and sit next to me."

The child hesitated, wiping his cheeks with his sleeve before uncrossing his legs and scooting to her side.

Meg's arms closed around him, holding him in a tight embrace. She tilted her head and rested her cheek on the top of his head. "Tell me what's worrying you, sweetie."

"I didn't pull any cat's tail." The words burst from his lips and his whole body shuddered. "I'm *not* a bad boy."

"It's just a game—" Cole began, wanting to console the boy, but Meg shook her head, a warning in her eyes.

"I don't want you and Uncle Cole to leave me." Charlie sniffed.

"I'm not going to leave you," Cole said, with a fierceness that took him by surprise. "Ever."

Cole could almost feel Dr. Allman standing over him, shaking his head in disapproval. Okay, so maybe he could have used this as a teaching moment to explain the life cycle to the child, but right now, Cole sensed Charlie needed reassurance, not more rhetoric.

"I'm not leaving, either." Meg met the boy's gaze, her eyes golden in the lamplight. "But I'd like to know what you think can happen when a little boy or girl is naughty."

Soft as silk, Meg's tone invited confidence.

"Sometimes they have to clean up the mess," Charlie whispered.

"That's true." Meg nodded. "What else?"

"They have to say they're sorry."

"Also true." Meg gave the boy's shoulder a reassuring squeeze.

Cole resisted the urge to interrupt and tell Charlie that every adult knew that being naughty was simply part of being a child. Reiterate that this was only a game and sooner or later he and Meg would land on the same type of square. But he didn't say a word. From the look on her face, it was obvious Meg had a plan.

Charlie stuck his thumb in his mouth and began to suck, his head now resting against Meg's chest.

Cole's heart clenched. Dr. Allman had spoken with him and Meg before Charlie's session and told them that behavioral regression after a sudden loss was common. Apparently sucking his thumb was his son's way of comforting himself.

Still, knowing Charlie was in such pain that he had to revert to such childish behavior to find comfort brought tears to Cole's eyes. He hurriedly blinked them back, hoping no one had noticed.

Charlie was staring into space and Meg's full attention appeared focused on the boy. She stroked his hair and murmured soothing sounds.

"What else, sweetie?" she asked, her voice low. "What else do you think happens when you do something bad?"

For a moment it appeared the child might not respond. Then he lifted his head and pulled the thumb from his mouth.

Cole smiled encouragingly, wanting the boy to know he had his support. But Charlie's eyes remained downcast.

"They go away and never come back."

Charlie mumbled the words, but they were still loud enough to hear.

"Who—?"

"Had you gotten into trouble the morning of the car accident?" Meg asked.

Cole now understood where she was headed and he didn't like it one bit. The question made it sound as if she thought the child had some culpability.

"I left my toys out and Mommy tripped and fell." Charlie's chin trembled. "She cried. Daddy was mad at me."

"What did he do?" Meg's expression held no condemnation, only curiosity.

"He hugged Mommy until she stopped crying then told me I couldn't play with my dinosaurs the rest of the week." The boy chewed on his lower lip. "Daddy and I picked up the toys so no one else would get hurt. But they did. They both got hurt."

"Your parents were killed in a car accident, son. It didn't have anything to do with the toys on the floor. They didn't want to leave you," Cole said. "Your mommy and daddy loved you very much."

Charlie glanced at Meg.

"Uncle Cole is right," she said. "Do you remember what happened that day?"

The child slowly nodded. "A big truck hit our car."

"That's right." Meg gently pushed a stray strand of hair back from his face. "The driver of the truck had been drinking alcohol and he weaved into your daddy's lane. There was no time for your car to get out of the way."

"I want Mommy. I want Daddy." Tears ran down Charlie's cheeks and he popped the thumb back into his mouth.

"I know you do." Meg's eyes filled with tears and this time she let them fall. "You loved them and they loved you very, very much. Every time I came to visit, that's what they both told me."

"But Mommy fell down," Charlie insisted. "She cried."

"I bet when she got into the car she wasn't crying," Meg said, her lips curving up, a smile of remembrance in her eyes. "Your mommy loved car rides."

"She was happy," Charlie said. "We were singing when…"

His small voice trailed off.

Cole thought back to those days he and Joy had spent together in Austin. He'd almost forgotten how she liked to sing along with the radio while they were driving down the road. Tears stung the backs of his lids.

Joy would be so distressed that Charlie, her beloved son, carried around guilt over something that was outside of his control.

For the first time Cole understood how different it was to have a parent die suddenly. At least with his father's death, they'd had time to prepare and no words had been left unsaid. "If your mom was sitting with us now, what do you think she'd say to you?"

Perhaps it wasn't the right thing to ask, but he was flying blind here.

The boy thought for a moment then sat up straight.

"She'd say, 'Charlie, why are you crying?'" His tone mimicked his mother's perfectly. "And I'd say, 'Because I miss you, Mommy.'"

Meg's eyes filled with tears.

"I'd tell her," Charlie continued, "that I want her and Daddy back here with me."

"You know they'd be here if they could," Cole said. "My dad didn't want to die and leave my brother and me. Aunt Meg's mom and dad died on that same road where your parents had their accident. They didn't want to leave her, either."

Charlie thought for a moment. "I bet they're happy now."

Meg cocked her head.

"'Cause they can see us eating popcorn and playing games. They know we're not alone anymore."

Out of the mouth of babes…

Cole swallowed the lump that rose to his throat. On his deathbed, his dad had told him and his brother that he would always be in their back pockets. That no matter where he went or what happened, he would be with them.

It was a good thought, but Cole had longed for an earthly

father. Someone to play ball with him and come to his games. Someone to guide and support him as he grew up.

Losing a parent could be devastating, but at least Charlie wasn't alone. Charlie had him. God willing, would always have him.

Cole's gaze drifted to where Meg sat, an arm looped around his son's shoulders, smiling at something the child had said.

In that moment Cole knew Charlie had been right. He had no doubt that Ty and Joy were looking down from heaven, grateful that their son had found a home with two people who loved him. Which meant severing all ties with Meg once he gained full custody was no longer an option.

For Charlie's sake, Meg would have to remain in the little boy's life.

Consequently, she would remain in his, as well.

Chapter Ten

By the time Charlie fell asleep, exhaustion had wrapped itself around Meg's shoulders like a heavy shawl. Since the child's room was only a couple doors down the hall from hers, she was tempted to go straight to bed.

The only thing that stopped her from doing just that was the knowledge that Cole was still up. He'd tucked in Charlie then headed downstairs ostensibly to get some ibuprofen for his aching knee.

Meg knew that had been a ruse, a ploy to give her more time alone with the boy, in case there was anything Charlie needed to share before he drifted off to sleep.

But Meg knew Charlie was done talking about his parents, at least for the evening. About an hour before bedtime, Cole had pulled out a box of action figures and from that point on Charlie's whole focus had been on Castle Grayskull and the Masters of the Universe action figures.

Meg thought it was cool knowing these were the same

toys Cole had played with when he'd been Charlie's age. Though they'd tried to give her the Man-at-Arms action figures, being therapeutic and empathetic for much of the evening had sucked the energy right out of her. She'd been content to watch Cole and his new son play with Skeletor and He-Man.

It had felt good to simply chill and regroup. She'd been a little over her head today. When Charlie had begun to confide his fears, she'd immediately begun to worry. What if she said the wrong thing and traumatized the child more? She'd hoped Cole would jump in, but it quickly became apparent he was yielding to her expertise.

Meg snorted. As if being the oldest girl in a family of eight children or raising teenagers had given her extra insight into a small boy's brain.

Still, Charlie *had* gone to sleep with a smile on his face. Unfortunately, Meg now faced an even more daunting task—dealing with Cole and THE OFFER.

The way they'd left it made it appear she was considering his proposition. Which she wasn't. What he had proposed was totally out of the question. That was the reason she aimed her feet toward the stairs. She needed to set the record straight.

And she must do it now…before she convinced herself that having an affair with Cole Lassister made some sort of crazy sense.

Cole looked up from the magazine he'd been flipping through when he heard Meg's footsteps on the stairs. The chill he'd felt when he'd shut off the fireplace turned to heat the second he turned his head and saw her.

Her red-brown curls lay in a tangled mess around her shoulders. Sometime during the evening she'd shed her shoes and her lipstick. Still, even at the end of a long day, with fatigue bracketing her eyes, she remained a beautiful woman.

Of course, he knew lots of beautiful women.

He lifted a brow when she dropped into the chair opposite the sofa where he sat.

"Charlie asleep?" he asked, determined to keep the conversation neutral until he ascertained the reason for her late-night visit.

"Out like a light." She smiled and rested her head against the back of the chair. "I honestly believe this evening's discussion was harder on us than on him."

Cole had always known Meg was smart and had a quick mind. Tonight he'd seen her sensitive side. The way she'd comforted Charlie had been amazing. "You did a superb job of helping him understand that his parents didn't die because of anything he did."

"Thank you," Meg said, but worry still clouded her eyes. "I think he's doing okay. I hope he is."

He placed the magazine on the coffee table. "How about you?"

"What do you mean?"

"Is parenthood what you thought it would be? How are you holding up?"

"Despite the challenges, I'm liking it." Meg leaned forward, resting her arms on her thighs.

The V-neck of her sweater gaped, giving Cole a good view of the swells of her breasts. Suddenly, talking no longer seemed quite so important. He swallowed past the dryness in his throat.

"As much as I initially didn't want to live under the same roof with you," she continued, "I'm happy it worked out this way."

"Because you get to see me every day at my best?" He kept his tone light, though his eyes never left hers.

He didn't flinch when her gaze took in his hair that was probably going in all directions. He even managed to hold steady when she let her gaze linger on his cheeks, which had to be dark with stubble by now.

"That's definitely part of it." Her lips curved into a slight smile. "But it's not the number one benefit."

Meg moistened her lips with her tongue, and his body surged in response. Was she speaking in cryptic terms of their time on the bed? He wondered why she didn't just come out and say being in the same house would make it much easier for them to sleep togeth—

"Having the chance to coparent with you on a day-to-day basis has been the real blessing."

What? Whoa. Coparenting?

This had to be some sort of joke.

"I'd forgotten what a nice guy you are." A dusky pink settled on her cheeks. "Living here has shown me what a good father you'll be."

Though Cole had told himself he didn't care what she thought of him—what she'd ever thought of him—the satisfaction surging through his veins told him he did.

"I—I think if we'd immediately set up separate households, it wouldn't have been good for Charlie. I think seeing us getting along is helping him cope." She straightened, the soft fabric of the sweater now hugging her large breasts.

Cole pulled his gaze away and cleared his throat, trying to decipher what she was really saying. Something about getting along was good for Charlie.

Admittedly, she'd fallen into the mother role with an ease he envied. And Charlie seemed to like her. "I agree."

He thought of the DNA test kit that had come in the mail today and was now safely ensconced in his dresser drawer. Cole planned to do the test as soon as Meg was out running errands and he was alone with Charlie. Once the results came back and he could prove the boy was his biological child, his attorneys had the papers ready to petition for sole guardianship.

Cole was still determined to continue with that plan. This ease between him and Meg changed nothing. Still, seeing how Charlie responded to her made him realize that cutting her completely out of his life might not be best for the boy. She would need to retain some role in his son's life.

But what kind of role should that be? Contemplating the question made his head hurt.

A song playing on the radio in the background caught his ear. While checking out local country stations, he'd come across the one he'd always listened to when he'd been in high school.

Cole reached over and turned up the volume, then pushed himself to a standing position and held out a hand. "Care to dance?"

"What? Why?" she asked, yet rose to her feet without waiting for an answer.

"The station is playing hits from the late nineties tonight." His hand closed over hers and he pulled her into his arms. They touched from chest to thighs, but by the time she opened her mouth to tell him she couldn't dance, they were swaying to a romantic ballad tailor-made for slow dancing. "This song was number one on the charts the spring of our junior year."

"How do you remember that?" She tilted her head as they moved side-to-side in a sensual rhythm.

Cole tried not to think about how good she felt in his arms.

"I've a good memory for songs," he said simply. It was the truth, just not the whole truth.

They'd been seeing each other only a short time when he'd started saving his money. He'd planned to ask Meg to the junior-senior prom. Each time he heard a slow song on the radio he imagined himself holding her body close as they danced under the glittering mirror ball in the high school gymnasium.

Thankfully he'd found out what she really thought of him before he asked her. No one saw his disappointment. Living with a mean drunk had taught him the art of hiding his emotions.

Though Cole had told himself he no longer cared what Meg did or with whom, as the date for the big event drew near, he'd found himself wondering whose arms she'd be in that night. He'd concluded it would be Ed Rice. The guy followed her around like a lovesick puppy.

Then her parents had been killed. Neither she nor Travis went to prom that year. And once the school year ended, they were gone.

"Do you know I never went to a single high school dance?" Meg closed her eyes and rested her head against his shoulder.

"That's hard to believe." He tightened his arms around her. "You were so beautiful."

The compliment came out before he could stop it.

Meg laughed as if he'd made a joke. "Give it up, Lassiter. Back then *no one,* including you, thought I was beautiful."

"I always told you how beautiful you were."

"Yes, you did," she conceded, but there was a disturbing edge to her tone. "Back then you said a lot of things that weren't true. Lies geared toward getting me in the backseat of your Chevy."

Cole narrowed his gaze. "Lies?"

"I'm simply stating facts." Meg pushed him away and

took a step back. "You showered me with compliments and told me how much you cared. After we made love, you dropped me. A girl doesn't need a degree in mathematics to come to that conclusion."

Cole couldn't believe it. She was attempting to make *him* out to be the bad guy in their breakup.

"When I gave you that locket for Valentine's Day—" Cole paused, feeling the muscle in his jaw jump "—I meant every word."

"You didn't return my phone calls. You ignored me at school. It was as if I didn't exist. Those aren't the actions of a boy in love." She gave a humorless laugh. "Of course you said you loved me. You might have even believed it. What hormone-ridden high school boy hasn't used those words to get into a girl's pants?"

"Believe what you want." With his jaw set in a hard angle, he jerked her back against him. Despite a twinge in his knee, he executed a series of turns that left her breathless.

"What I want is answers," Meg said.

"Really?" he said between gritted teeth. "Appears to me you think you've got it all figured out."

"I want to know why you stopped calling. One day we were the perfect couple. The next day you acted like you didn't know me."

The perfect couple? This time it was his turn to laugh. She hadn't even wanted anyone to know they were dating.

It had been the first of many clues he'd missed. She'd insisted they keep their "relationship" from her family and friends. She'd given him some bull about it being more special when it was their little secret. He realized now that she'd been embarrassed.

He came from the wrong side of the tracks. He hadn't been in the accelerated classes like all her friends. Honor roll? He'd been lucky to maintain the C average he needed for football.

Perhaps Cole should have told her that he *knew* she'd betrayed his trust and told Ed he couldn't read well. Yet, merely recalling that time brought back a flood of painful memories and feelings he'd done his best to forget. The past was the past, he told himself. It couldn't be changed.

For Charlie's sake, they needed to move on.

"We were young. We made mistakes," Cole said when he realized Meg was waiting for a reply. "I don't know about you, but I look back on that time with a whole litany of regrets."

Regrets like he wished he'd set out for Texas the day he'd gotten his driver's license. Meeting and moving in with his uncle had changed the course of his life. If only he'd done it sooner.

He wished he'd slugged Ed Rice. Though he firmly believed violence was rarely the answer, wiping that smirk off Ed's lips with his fist would have been worth the fall-out.

Most of all, he wished he'd never gotten involved with Meg.

With his hand on the small of her back, he steered her with gentle caresses to the beat of the music. Considering his knee, he made a surprisingly good dance partner.

"I have regrets, too," Meg admitted after a long moment.

She thought about her parents and how she'd lied to them about her relationship with Cole. She hadn't wanted anyone to know they were dating because deep in her heart she'd known the relationship wouldn't last. He was the handsome football star every girl wanted to date. She was the red-haired science geek who'd never even kissed a boy.

She wished she hadn't believed Cole when he said he

loved her. Most of all, she wished she'd never gotten involved with him.

"We could start over," he said in an offhand tone as if it didn't matter to him one way or another. "Pretend we've just met."

Meg could see where he was going with this. He was asking a lot. Yet, he *had* been only a boy when he'd treated her so badly. Since she'd been back in Jackson Hole, she'd seen no evidence of that callous youth in the man he'd become. Though he hadn't openly apologized, at least he had admitted he had regrets over how he'd behaved.

"I'm game if you are," she said finally.

For Charlie's sake, she told herself. She was doing this for Charlie's sake.

Meg prayed that was true. Because if it wasn't, she could be headed for big trouble.

Chapter Eleven

"Now that we've settled one aspect of our relationship, I want—" Cole took a step back and held Meg at arm's length "—to talk about the proposition still on the table."

Meg could feel her face warm even as her eyes, which seemed to have suddenly developed a mind of their own, zeroed in on the area directly below his belt buckle.

"I've thought about it," she said quickly. "I don't think us becoming physically…intimate would be wise."

She lifted her gaze. The eye contact quickly turned into something more, a tangible connection between the two of them.

"Then I'll settle for another dance." He tugged her back into his arms, placing his hands on her hips while she reluctantly twined her fingers behind his neck.

To be so close didn't seem prudent, especially considering what had happened on his bed earlier. Yet to refuse seemed…childish. After all, it wasn't as if she was afraid of him.

More like afraid of myself, Meg thought with a wry smile.

"It'll be like we're dancing at prom," she murmured, finding comfort in the words. After all, kids went to such events in high school all the time. Those nights rarely ended with the couple having sex. "Dancing should be safe."

Even as she reassured herself, Meg shivered with desire. The mere feel of his body against hers brought a fresh rush of longing.

"Safe?" Cole chuckled, a low, pleasant rumbling sound. "If you say so."

"I can't deny that your offer is tempting," she said slowly. "But we have to be smart about this."

His hand, which had begun to caress her back while they moved in time to the music, stilled. "You think I'm stupid?"

There was an edge to his tone that she didn't understand. Meg tilted her head back and met his gaze. "I was simply saying that becoming physically involved when we're trying to find our way in our relationship with each other and with Charlie could be problematic."

Chuckling, Cole kissed the corner of her mouth. "It's such a turn-on when you talk like a schoolteacher."

Though warning bells went off in her head, Meg had to laugh. "What am I going to do with you?"

"Kiss me," he whispered, the tip of his tongue circling her ear. "One kiss."

A smoldering heat flared through her at his suggestion, scaring and thrilling her at the same time.

"One kiss?" She spoke then paused, not sure what she wanted.

"That will be the plan," he said in a nonchalant tone. "But if you change your mind and want more, we don't have to stop at one."

One little peck on the lips. What would be the harm?

Still, Meg hesitated.

"You want to kiss me," he said, his voice a husky caress. "True? Or false?"

"True," she reluctantly admitted.

"And I want to kiss you. In fact, right now I'm finding it hard to think of anything else."

Time seemed to stretch and extend. The music took on a seductive beat. Do it. Do it, the pulsating rhythm urged.

"C'mon, Meg," he murmured, twining strands of her hair loosely around his fingers. "One little kiss for your prom date."

After the tiniest hesitation she nodded. Anticipation fluttered through her.

One kiss, she told herself, *maybe two.*

He caught her hand in his, brought it to his mouth and pressed a kiss in the palm.

She pulled her brows together. "That's it?"

Cole laughed. "You are so demanding."

He lowered his head and kissed her softly, gently, while Richard Marx began to sing in the background. Cole's lips were warm and sweet and Meg let her eyelids flutter shut, savoring the closeness.

The music transported her to a high school gym decorated with crepe streamers and balloons. Cole was in a tux and she was in a slinky dress that made her look beautiful and they were kissing on the dance floor.

He continued pressing his lips lightly to hers, teasingly, his mouth never pulling away. His hands slipped underneath her sweater, slowly sliding up and down her back.

When his thumbs skimmed the edges of her breasts,

Meg waited for his fingers to try to unclasp her bra—not that she would allow that liberty, of course—but he lowered his hands to her waist and simply continued to kiss her.

After a moment, she gave in to temptation and wrapped her arms more tightly around his neck, dragging him closer, drinking him in.

When they finally came up for air, she leaned her forehead against his. "That's one."

Cole's brow lifted.

"Our lips stayed connected," Meg said, trying not to sound defensive. "That makes it one kiss."

His mouth—that wonderful, delightful mouth—widened into a smile. "I like the way you count."

She played with the strands of his hair, her breath coming in short puffs. Dear God, if she got this excited over kissing the man, what would it be like if they made love? *No need to go there,* she told herself. Her body unfortunately seemed to have developed a mind of its own.

"The kiss helped. My thoughts are clearer," he said. "I now see why you think making love would be a mistake."

"Really?" Was that disappointment she heard in her voice?

His gaze turned sharp and assessing. Finally a slow smile lifted his lips. "Actually, no. I believe I need another kiss before I come to such an important conclusion."

Meg knew he was teasing her but she didn't care. She wanted another kiss. And another. And maybe one more for good measure.

"Perhaps—" she brought a finger to the lips that still tingled from his touch "—taking the kiss a little...deeper might help offer some clarity."

His eyes danced. "Let's give it a try."

Without waiting for her response, Cole tilted her head

back, teasing the fullness of her lower lip with his tongue. He tasted like the most delicious, decadent candy Meg had ever eaten.

She parted her lips and he immediately changed the angle of the kiss and plunged inside, claiming her mouth. His tongue circled and danced with hers. She did the same to him, each touch, each tingle reinforcing the possibilities.

Her fingers trembled as she caressed his face, his hair. Her head spun. If he hadn't been holding her so tight she'd have lost her footing.

Then suddenly the kiss ended and her head was on his shoulder. The only thing she was aware of was the beating of her heart mingled with his.

Two kisses. She'd promised herself she'd stop at two. Or was it three?

A sigh escaped her lips.

"Hey." He tipped her head back with a curled finger, his blue eyes dark and filled with concern. "What's wrong?"

Meg thought of the weeks, months and maybe even years that had been filled with regret over what could have been. Sure, she'd survived and had moved on with her life. Still, every now and then she hadn't been able to stop herself from looking back. Even at sixteen, she'd recognized that the relationship between her and Cole was special. She'd firmly believed that, given the right time and place, they could have gone the distance.

"Meg?" he prompted.

It all became clear. She and Cole had been given a second chance.

She was apprehensive, of course. After how their relationship had ended before, who wouldn't be? But a lot had happened in both their lives since that time.

Meg understood Cole better now than she had back then.

"You're so beautiful," he said.

"Flattery," she said slowly and distinctly so there could be no misunderstanding, "will get you everything."

He cocked his head. "Every*thing?*"

The rightness of the decision washed over her. "We can discuss this further at your place."

There was a beat of silence. Confusion filled his gaze. "Uh, this *is* my place."

Meg giggled. Honest to goodness giggled. If she hadn't heard it herself she'd never have believed it. "Your place, as in *your bedroom.*"

In case she still hadn't made herself clear, Meg pulled his face down with her hand and gave him a ferocious kiss. The type of kiss that tells a man "I want you now."

She'd learned long ago that regret over something you wished you'd said or done but no longer had the chance to do was its own kind of hell. And she wasn't letting this opportunity pass her by.

Cole seemed equally determined to seize the moment. He locked his hand around her elbow and propelled her into the bedroom, only stopping to close and lock the door behind them.

Usually Meg was the poster child of calm, but tonight she was a tangled mess of wants and desires. Her need for him a stark carnal hunger she hadn't known she was capable of feeling.

"This better not take too long or I'm going to combust," she murmured and felt some of her nervousness fade at his quick laughter.

"I'm afraid I'm going to do my best to stoke that fire," he said in a husky voice that made her blood feel like warm honey sliding through her veins. "But I promise if we go up in flames it will be together."

Cole moved his arm so her hand slid down to his and he gently locked their fingers together, tugging her to the bed. Once there, he pulled her up against him, linking his arms lightly around her waist.

A sudden look of tenderness crossed his face. His grin was a little lopsided, his fingers not quite steady as they touched the curve of her cheek and trailed along the line of her jaw.

"You won't regret this," he said and his voice was like a promise.

Meg met his gaze. Could he hear her heart pounding? When he looked in her eyes, could he see her desire reflecting back at him?

Once again he seemed to know what she was thinking. He began to remove his clothing, cursing when his hands fumbled with the brace. She shrugged out of her dress, letting the soft fabric fall to the floor before unfastening the last of the Velcro straps for him with shaking hands.

In a matter of seconds, their clothes lay in a pile at their feet and Cole's gaze was riveted to her now-bare breasts. But thankfully he wasn't content to look and not touch. His long fingers lifted and supported the yielding flesh as his thumbs brushed across the tight points of her nipples.

Shock waves coursed through her body with each touch. Moaning, she reached out and wrapped her hand around his hardness.

"I have protection," he groaned, gesturing with a short jerk of his head toward the dresser.

"I've got it covered," she managed to say.

"Yes, you do." A tiny smile touched his lips as he glanced at her fingers stroking him.

He couldn't seem to get enough of her breasts, kissing and licking each pink peak thoroughly, dragging his teeth across the sensitive skin.

Meg squirmed, whimpering in frustration. She pushed

her hips against him, rubbing his erection. She wanted, no, she needed…

Cole's answer to her unspoken demand was to catch her mouth in a hard, deep kiss and pull her down beside him on the bed. His hand flattened against her lower back, drawing her up against the length of his body.

Conscious of his knee, Meg draped herself across him, body on body, his arousal pressing into her thigh while she rubbed herself against him, her breath coming in short puffs.

While she wanted to prolong the pleasure, she couldn't wait. Running her hands up his chest, she pushed him back down, guiding him inside her as he nuzzled her breasts. He was thick and hard and stretched her to perfection.

She moved her hips against his in a sensual rhythm as old as time, shivers of desire traveling up and down her spine. Cole held on to her hips, guiding her up and down in a steady rhythm she couldn't resist.

Just when she thought she couldn't stand any more pleasure, he captured her mouth in a deep, hot, tongue-tangling kiss that mimicked the fast, hard, frantic mating of their bodies. Meg surged against the pleasure swelling like the tide inside her.

Her body trembled and she tried to hold on, but he continued to pump his hips up and down, again and again, every thrust harder than the one before until she cried out, her body convulsing around his shaft, milking him, shuddering with the force of her own release.

Cole opened his eyes the next morning to the feel of Meg's soft lips against his neck. He stretched and slid a hand up her bare arm. "Now, this is the way every day should begin."

Meg chuckled and rested her head against his shoulder,

her fingers toying with the hair on his chest. When she brushed the small bud of his nipple, Cole's breath hissed between his teeth and his body jolted.

"It's only six—" she found his other nipple buried in the curling mat of hair and rubbed her thumb over the tight bud, the edge of her nail scraping ever so lightly "—and I thought if we were really quick we might have time—"

A wave of heat swept through him. "I like the way you think."

Reaching up, he grasped her arms and pulled her to him for an openmouthed, intimate kiss. Though they'd already made love several times during the night, he was ready to do it again.

"I like the way you kiss." Meg let her head fall back, baring her neck and throat to his lips, a purr of pleasure rumbling in her throat.

"The way you smell drives me crazy," he said, nuzzling her ear and kissing her neck.

Cole brushed the hair back from her face with a gentle hand then kissed her with an intensity that had them both breathing hard in seconds.

With a low groan, he pulled her on top of him. As much as he'd have liked to have mixed up the positions, for now his knee limited the possibilities. Still, that didn't mean they couldn't have fun....

His hips surged upward, his mind conjuring up images of naked limbs entwined, of his body filling her as he thrust hard and deep. His hand had slipped downward, to the part of her that was already swollen with need, when he heard the noise.

From Meg's sudden stiffening, she'd heard it, too.

A knock. And then another.

"Uncle Cole." Charlie's voice sounded from the other side of the locked door. "Can I come in?"

For a second, Cole froze.

Meg gasped and rolled off of him. She grabbed a corner of the sheet, attempting to cover herself as if she feared Charlie would come storming into the room any second.

"The door is locked," he mouthed, finding reassurance in the knowledge.

"What's wrong, bud?" Even as he forced a calm tone, Cole swung his legs over to the side of the bed and stood, quickly shuffling his way to the closet. He began tossing on clothes, conscious of Meg doing the same thing behind him.

"I can't find Aunt Meg," Charlie wailed, pounding on the door. "I think she left us."

"She didn't leave," Cole called back.

"How do you know?" The little boy whimpered.

Cole turned to see Meg kick her bra and panties beneath the bed and straighten her dress.

"Because she's here with me," Cole answered.

"I didn't go anywhere, Charlie," Meg called out. She surveyed Cole's running pants and T-shirt then gave a short nod of approval. "I got up early to help Uncle Cole with his exercises."

Jerking the comforter up over the tangled sheets, Cole took a seat on the edge of the bed then gestured to Meg to open the door.

"I'm sorry I worried you, sweetie." She opened the door, and his son, still in his firefighter fleece footie pajamas, fell into her open arms with a sob.

Cole's heart clenched at the tearstained face.

"I went to your room." The little boy hugged her tight, his voice thick with tears. "But you weren't there. I looked in the kitchen but you weren't there, either."

Meg stroked the top of Charlie's head. "I'm sorry, baby. Aunt Meg just didn't think you'd be up so early."

Over the child's head, her gaze met Cole's and her lips lifted in a rueful smile. Today they'd both learned a valuable lesson, one that undoubtedly countless parents had discovered before them.

No time was a completely safe time for sex. Not with a child in the house.

"Why *are* you up so early?" Cole asked. "Do you feel okay?"

Charlie tilted his head back, his eyes still shiny with tears.

"Today is the party," the child said as if that explained everything. He turned back to Meg. "Didn't you tell him?"

"Of course she did," Cole said immediately. He thought for a split second. "That's why I asked Aunt Meg to help me with my exercises this morning. I wanted to make sure my leg is in tip-top shape for the party tonight."

It was a pitiful excuse but the best Cole could think of on short notice.

Charlie nodded solemnly, seeming to accept the explanation. "Did Aunt Meg make it all better?"

Cole resisted the urge to look at Meg. "You know…it *is* better now."

"I can get on my clothes real fast. Then can we go?" Charlie wrenched himself from Meg's arms, no trace of the tears remaining. "I want to play with Connor and Caleb."

Travis's mischievous twin boys were in Charlie's first-grade class, and they, along with their parents and three other siblings, would be at the party tonight.

"We won't be leaving for the Delacourts' house until five," Meg explained.

"Five o'clock is a long time away," Cole stressed, wanting to make sure Charlie understood they wouldn't be getting into the car anytime soon.

Charlie looked abashed for a second then began hop-ping from one foot to the other. "Can we have pancakes for breakfast?"

Cole stifled a yawn, wondering how anyone could have such energy before the sun had been given a chance to rise. Of course, he'd probably be more ready to embrace the day if he'd slept more than a few hours last night.

"Can we have pancakes, Aunt Meg?" Charlie repeated when she didn't immediately answer. "Please?"

"Of course." Meg smiled. "Uncle Cole and I picked up some chocolate chips when we were at the store. You can toss a few into the batter, if you'd like. But first you have to wash your hands."

"I'll wash 'em right now." Without another word, Charlie galloped from the room.

"With soap," Meg called after him.

Cole raised a brow. "Chocolate-chip pancakes?"

"If you don't like them, we can make some without the chips." Meg bent to reach under the bed. She pulled out a white lace bra and matching panties then dropped them into his top dresser drawer. "I'll be back later to retrieve these."

"Be sure to come when you have time to stay and... visit."

For a second she hesitated, and he feared she was going to say that last night was a one-time event and she'd gotten him out of her system.

Instead she grinned. "Absolutely."

As she sauntered to the door with her hips swaying from side to side, Cole realized two important facts.

One, a single night with her hadn't been enough. If anything, it had only increased his desire for her.

Two, she wasn't wearing any underwear beneath that dress.

He wasn't sure which fact caused him the most distress.

Chapter Twelve

There was no denying it. The Delacourt home in the mountains just outside of Jackson had been transformed into a winter wonderland. When Meg turned into the circular drive in front of the large stone-and-wood house, she had to smile at Charlie's excited shriek.

Meg was equally impressed. By the brightly colored lights decorating the snow-covered trees and shrubs. By the antique sleigh filled with lit packages of every shape and color. Even by the simple evergreen wreath with a big red bow hanging on the front door.

Her family had never done much in the way of decorating for the holidays. Merely shopping for gifts for eight children had taken most of her mom and dad's spare time. Yet Meg had yearned for a home filled with wreaths, garland and a tree with all the trimmings.

Decorating her own apartment had always seemed like

too much work for only one person to enjoy. Next year, though, she would do it. For Charlie. And for herself.

This year she vowed to make the holidays special for the little boy who now proudly carried her food offering to the house.

Nick and Lexi, along with their daughters, Addie and Grace, greeted them at the door, taking their coats and thanking them for the relish tray before pointing them in the direction of the great room.

As she and Cole and Charlie passed from one room to another, Meg quickly discovered the holiday decorations hadn't been confined to the exterior of the home. Sugar-coated gingerbread candles greeted them with a delicious scent when they stepped into the hall. Mistletoe hung over every doorway.

In the great room a collection of old-world Santas marched across the mantel while orange flames danced in the hearth. A large fir tree, decorated with garlands of cranberries and popcorn, stopped just shy of the twenty-foot ceiling.

A sumptuous spread had been set buffet-style on a large table. Covered in a red tablecloth, a thick gold velvet ribbon had been wrapped around the upper sides of the table and tied in bows. Small evergreen wreaths hung at regular intervals, providing a hint of color.

Charlie loved it. Or at least he loved the light coat of gold glitter over the top of the table. She and Cole simply exchanged smiles when the boy insisted it was "real" gold but didn't attempt to correct him.

Mary Karen, her sister-in-law, strolled over at that point, one of her baby twins on her hip. Dressed in a form-fitting red sweater dress, Meg would never have known she was the mother of five.

"Hi, M.K.," Meg said, using her brother's nickname for

his wife. She glanced around the room. "I don't know why but for some reason I thought this was a sit-down dinner."

"That was how it was initially planned, but we all thought a buffet would be better." Mary Karen paused to disentangle several long blond strands of hair from her daughter's chubby fingers. "Look at the selection. Everyone should be able to find something they like."

Mary Karen widened her smile to include Cole and explained that after choosing from a wide array of gourmet foods, the adults could take their plates to any number of tables scattered throughout the main level of the house. A "children's table" had been stationed in the kitchen. Lexi and Nick had hired a couple of high school girls to supervise the children, leaving the parents free to mingle.

Her sister-in-law then turned her attention to Charlie. Meg hadn't been sure how the boy would react to leaving her side. Once again he surprised her. When Mary Karen asked if he'd like to sit at a table with her three boys and have some "creamy cola spider," Charlie immediately put his hand in hers and waved a cheery goodbye to Meg and Cole.

"Makes me feel important." Cole chuckled and rested a hand against the small of Meg's back.

"It only gets worse," Meg said in a light tone, doing her best to ignore the heat radiating from his touch. The fact that the tantalizing scent of his spicy cologne surrounded her only made it that much more difficult to focus.

"Wait until he's a teenager," she finally managed to stammer. "I guarantee there will be times when he won't even want to be seen with you because he's afraid you'll do or say something to embarrass him."

"Sounds like you speak from experience." Cole slanted a sideways glance. "But you're not that much older than your

youngest sibling. I can't imagine any of them not wanting
to show off their beautiful older sister."

Meg met his gaze, knowing he had to be teasing. After
all, he had to remember how gawky and awkward she'd
been back then. The look of admiration in his eyes took
her by surprise.

"Trust me," she said when she finally found her voice.
"To a sixteen-year-old brother, a twenty-two-year-old sister
is ancient. Zac was absolutely mortified each time I was
called to his school because of something he'd done."

"Zac?" Cole cocked his head. "He's the youngest."

"That's right," Meg said, surprised he remembered. It
wasn't like he'd ever been over to the house or formally
introduced to her family. The realization gave her a momentary twinge. "Zac and Ian are actually twins. Although
they're identical in looks, on the inside they're as different
as night and day."

Cole took two Candy Cane Swirl martinis from a passing waiter and handed one to Meg. "How so?"

"Ian always knew he wanted to be a mechanical engineer and he made that happen." Meg took a sip of the
drink and realized the tension that had once existed between her and Cole had disappeared. They were having a
very nice conversation and she was enjoying it. "He never
gave Travis or me a moment's worry. Zac, on the other
hand, well, let's just say *trouble* could have been that boy's
middle name."

"Yet—" Cole cupped her elbow in a possessive gesture
as they strolled around the room "—I sense a particular
fondness for this bad-boy brother of yours."

Cole, Margaret realized, was very perceptive.

"I think all my siblings would agree there's something
special about him." Meg took another sip of her martini,
savoring the delicious blend of peppermint schnapps and

vodka. "He's creative and talented. And despite his sometimes cocky exterior, Zac has a good heart."

"Where does he live?"

"Actually, that's a rather interesting sto—"

"I was hoping I'd run into the two of you tonight," Ryan
interrupted, a pretty dark-haired woman at his side. "I have
someone I'd like you to meet."

For the party, Meg had chosen a nubby wool skirt with
a green cashmere sweater. With snow on the ground and
more predicted over the course of the evening, she'd for-
gone pumps for heeled boots. When she'd glanced in the
mirror before leaving home she thought she looked stylish, even pretty. Cole's eyes had widened when he'd seen
her. A low wolf whistle had even escaped his lips.

Yet, standing next to this slender beauty in her jersey
dress the color of silver haze and stilettos that showed off
long, shapely legs, Meg realized how Cinderella's ugly
stepsisters must have felt.

She listened as Ryan introduced his companion as Dr.
Kate McNeal, a local pediatrician. Kate's hair hung to her
shoulders in a sleek bob, jet-black and silky. Long dark
lashes framed hazel eyes. Tall and lean, she had a fashion
sense that made her look more like a model than a children's doctor.

The woman seemed pleasant enough, although her hand
appeared to linger a heartbeat too long when she shook
Cole's hand.

"I was sorry to hear about Joy and Ty," Kate said. "They
were nice people and such good parents. How is Charlie
coping?"

Something clicked in Meg's head. "You're Charlie's pediatrician. I remember Joy mentioning your name."

"Guilty as charged," Kate said with an easy smile. "I'd

love to continue seeing him. Unless you have someone else in mind?"

Meg opened her mouth to say that she and Cole hadn't gotten around to discussing the matter yet, but Cole spoke first.

"I think it'll be best to keep things as consistent as possible for him," he said. "You'll definitely be seeing him again."

A flicker of irritation swept up Meg's spine. Not that she disagreed with Cole or thought that they *should* change doctors. That wasn't the point. This was a decision they should have made together. Yet once again he'd made a unilateral decision, leaving her out of the equation.

"How long have you been practicing in Jackson Hole?" Meg kept her tone even and forced a smile, determined not to let her irritation show. After all, none of this was Dr. McNeal's fault. But once she and Cole were alone, they'd discuss *again* what coparenting meant.

"I've been here about a year and a half." A tiny smile hovered at the corner of Kate's lips. "Your brother was one of my first friends when I moved here."

Meg wondered what her sister-in-law thought of Travis's "friend." She couldn't wait to ask Mary Karen.

"Ryan was so sweet to ask me to come with him today. He—" Kate paused. Her gaze narrowed on *someone* or *something* behind Meg.

"Looks like Joel Dennes and his daughter, Chloe, have arrived," Ryan said. "Weren't you asking me if he'd be here, Kate? Well, there he is."

Meg and Cole turned as one. A dark-haired man stood chatting with Lexi and Nick. A gangly girl, who looked to be around eight or nine years old, stood at his side, shifting from one foot to the other.

The man was tall, well over six feet, with a muscular

body, unruly chestnut hair and rugged features. Like most of the guys at the party, he was dressed in casual pants, a dress shirt and blazer.

His daughter wore a red velvet dress and black patent-leather shoes. Even at this young age, she showed promise of great beauty. Her hair was darker than her father's and straight, the shiny strands hanging past her shoulders. From what Meg could see, her features were delicate, her frame willowy.

"I don't think I've met them yet," Meg said.

A thoughtful look crossed Cole's face. "I don't remember him from school."

"Joel didn't grow up around here," Ryan informed them. "He expanded his business and relocated here a couple of years ago."

"If you'll excuse me, I'm going to pop over and say hello." Kate's eyes glittered and there was a slight quiver to her voice.

Meg exchanged a look with Cole.

"I'll go with you," Ryan said, placing his drink on a nearby side table.

"Nonono." Kate lifted a hand and shook her head. "Stay and talk with your friends. I won't be long."

Giving Meg and Cole a distracted smile, she hurried off, tossing an "it was nice to meet you both" over her shoulder.

For a second an awkward silence descended over the threesome left behind.

"She's a beautiful woman," Cole said finally.

Meg felt a twinge of jealousy. Yes, she simply must remember to ask her sister-in-law about Kate McNeal.

"Kate is smart, pretty and a lot of fun," Ryan murmured, picking up the cocktail glass he'd just discarded and finishing off the drink. "She's the whole package."

"Have you been dating long?" Meg asked, not sure if she should ask the questions hovering on the tip of her tongue or change the subject. Curiosity won out.

"A couple months off and on," Ryan said, his eyes hooded. "Not exclusively. Kate doesn't seem interested in commitment."

When they moved off to the side to get out of the walkway, it conveniently gave them a better view of Kate and the father and daughter she'd hurried off to greet. The pretty doctor's face was animated and flushed, while the man's held only polite interest.

"Joel Dennes." Meg rolled the name around on her tongue. "The name is familiar. Isn't he the contractor who built my brother's new home?"

"That's him." Ryan took another drink from a passing waiter. "He also built this one."

"Sounds like he's doing well for himself," Meg said.

"He's doing pretty well for himself tonight, that's for sure." Cole gestured with his head toward Kate and her new BFFs. The pretty doctor's hand now rested on Joel's forearm. "Better watch out, Ry, or your date may end up going home with another man."

While they watched, Kate slipped her arm through Joel's and practically dragged him with her to the buffet table. Chloe disappeared into the kitchen with Lexi.

"I think his daughter may be one of Kate's patients." Ryan's eyes never left his "date." "She's probably trying to make sure the girl and her dad feel comfortable. I don't think they know many people here."

"Whatever you say." Cole's expression turned serious. "Just keep your eyes wide open, my friend. Trust me. There's nothing worse than finding out you've been played for the fool because you ignored the signs that were there all along."

Something in Cole's tone told Meg that he'd been down that path himself. She wondered when he'd gotten hurt. Had it been in college? Or perhaps once he started his own business?

"Kate and I are just friends," Ryan snapped. "She can see whoever she wants."

"I didn't mean—" Cole began.

"Drop it, Lassiter," Ryan said through gritted teeth.

"I don't know about you two, but I'm hungry. Why don't we check out the food?" Meg tried to keep her tone matter-of-fact. "We can snag one of the round tables and save a place for Kate. And for Joel, too, if he'd like to join us."

Ryan paused for a moment then shrugged. "Okay by me."

When he turned and headed for the buffet table, Meg exchanged a worried glance with Cole.

He simply smiled and gestured for her to follow Ryan to the buffet table. Along the way Cole and Meg paused to speak with David Wahl and his wife, July.

David had been Travis's best friend since they'd been little boys and Meg regarded him as a brother.

"Charlie was telling some interesting stories in the kitchen." David's eyes held an impish gleam.

His wife elbowed him in the side.

"Ah, July." David leaned over and kissed the top of his wife's striking red hair. "It's not as if Trav won't give her a hard time. At least this way Margaret will be prepared."

Meg kept a smile on her lips even as her heart sank to the tip of her boots. If David thought Travis would be upset, this must be big. "What did Charlie say?"

"Nothing important." July's hand fluttered in a dismissive wave. "Something about you and Cole kissing just like his mom and dad used to kiss."

Though she didn't glance in his direction, Meg could feel Cole's eyes on her.

"Who was all in the kitchen when he made this declaration?" she asked, grateful her voice came out casual and offhand.

Though Meg wasn't ashamed of kissing Cole, she really hadn't wanted others knowing they were anything more than friends until she knew where she really stood with him.

"Just my troublemaking hubby and me." July shot David a wink. "And Travis and Mary Karen, of course."

Of course.

Meg stifled a sigh. Charlie might as well have put it up on a billboard. Then, she stopped herself. It was a kiss, for God's sake. Who cared? Besides, Travis better think twice about razzing her about something so mundane. After all, when he'd been single, it wasn't as if he'd spent his spare time in church praying.

"Of course, that wasn't the interesting part." David picked up two dinner plates, handing one to his wife. He shook his head and chuckled. "You should have seen your brother's face when Charlie mentioned Cole was lying on top of you at the time…keeping you warm."

"He said *what?*" Meg's voice rose then broke.

A sympathetic look crossed July's face. "I'm not looking forward to the day when our Adam turns into a little tell-all machine."

For a second Meg was struck dumb. She could hardly deny she'd kissed Cole. Or that he'd been on top of her. But nothing more had happened. *At least not that time.* Besides, they were both consenting adults.

She shifted her gaze to Cole and found him staring. Though he didn't appear particularly disturbed by Charlie making their little escapade on the bed public, there was a strange watchful look in his eyes.

Thankfully she was spared the need to answer when Lexi appeared. Once again Meg was struck by how stunning their hostess looked in her black dress and pearls.

"Lexi," Meg said immediately, seizing the opportunity to change the subject. "This is a lovely party."

"Yes, it is," Cole echoed. "Thanks for the invitation."

"I'm glad you're enjoying it." Lexi brushed back a strand of hair, her large diamond ring glittering in the candlelight. "Unfortunately, I'm afraid your evening with us is about to be cut short."

"You're kicking us out?" Meg said with a laugh.

"I wish you could stay." Lexi sighed. "You barely arrived and I was hoping for a chance to get better acquainted with both of you."

For the first time Meg noticed the lines of worry edging the social worker's eyes.

"Is there a problem?" Cole stepped closer to Meg's side.

"I'm afraid your boy, Charlie, is a bit under the weather." Lexi spoke quickly as if wanting to make sure she relayed all the facts before they began asking questions. "Travis thought he looked flushed, so we checked his temp. He's running a fever and his throat is bright red. Now he's saying his tummy hurts."

"Oh, my goodness." Panic rose up inside Meg, but she pushed it down, telling herself there was no need to worry. After all, he'd been fine an hour ago. "He was laughing and joking around all afternoon. No complaints at all."

Meg turned to Cole, seeking confirmation.

He nodded then focused on Lexi. "I hope you know we'd never have brought him tonight if we'd known he was sick."

"No worries." Lexi's understanding smile widened to

include Meg. "Almost everyone here has kids. We know how quickly illnesses pop up."

Apparently having overheard the discussion, David returned to join the group, a partially filled salad plate in one hand. "There's a nasty virus going around. Fever, headache, sore throat *and* gastrointestinal issues. It's been hanging on a good seventy-two hours. Very contagious."

"Does he need medical attention?" Cole asked.

"Well, it sounds as if Uncle Travis has already checked him out." David's lips tipped up in a wry smile. "But then again he is only an obstetrician."

Meg couldn't even manage a smile at the joke.

"Where is Charlie now?" Cole's tone might give nothing away, but Meg knew he was as worried as she.

"Rachel took him upstairs to rest in the spare bedroom while I came to get you." Lexi smiled reassuringly. "She's a nurse so he's in good hands."

Meg shifted her gaze to Cole. "How about I run upstairs and get him and we'll meet you in the foyer?"

By the look in his eyes and his hesitation, Meg knew he wanted desperately to head upstairs to check on Charlie himself. But while Cole was able to negotiate stairs, it was still a slow process. They both knew she could reach the boy in half the time. Which meant they could be on the road more quickly and Charlie could be home in his own bed that much sooner.

He thought for a second then nodded. "I'll get the coats and meet you at the front door."

Meg turned toward Lexi.

"Could you please take me to my—" she paused "—to Charlie?"

Meg had almost said "to my son." Though it had been only several weeks that she'd been fulfilling the mother role, she realized that's how she thought of Charlie now.

Her boy.

Her son.

Like countless mothers before her, she would willingly go to the ends of the earth to protect him.

From anything.

Or anyone.

Chapter Thirteen

Cole had just taken a sip of apple cider when he heard Meg's footsteps on the stairs.

He twisted his body and glanced over the top of the sofa. "How is he?"

"Asleep," she said with a weary smile, her arms filled with laundry. "Let me put his clothes in the washer and then I'll join you."

Cole had sat in the back of the SUV on the way home, talking to his son and trying to distract him. Thankfully Lexi and Nick's home was just down the road, so the trip went quickly.

With Kate's approval, Rachel had given Charlie some acetaminophen for his headache and fever before they'd left.

Cole had thought Charlie was feeling better until the boy stepped into the kitchen and upchucked everything he'd eaten all over himself, the countertop and the floor.

When Charlie began crying and apologizing, all at the same time, Cole's heart had overflowed with love. Even as he'd reassured his son "no harm, no foul," he wished Charlie would quit worrying that he and Meg would leave him.

While Meg took Charlie upstairs to clean him up and put him to bed—reassuring him with each step—Cole busied himself cleaning the kitchen. He may have gagged a couple of times, but he'd gotten it done. Once the onerous—not to mention odorous—task was accomplished, he'd heated up some apple cider, plopped a cinnamon stick in each cup and taken the cups into the living room.

Meg's voice sounded from the doorway. "Promise you'll let me know when you hear the washer alarm go off."

Cole looked up. Sometime between when she'd headed upstairs with Charlie and came back down with the laundry, she'd changed into an oversize T-shirt and sweatpants and pulled back her hair into a ponytail.

Though he'd thought she'd been the most beautiful woman at the party—he especially loved the way that soft sweater had clung to her curves—she appealed to him just as much now. Perhaps even more. Which made no sense at all.

"I don't want to forget to put Charlie's clothes in the dryer," she continued.

"Forget the laundry. It's time to party." Cole gestured to the mugs. "Hot apple cider for us. Once you assure me that our boy is fine."

A look that he couldn't immediately decipher crossed Meg's face. "*Our* boy?"

"Charlie," Cole clarified, though he wasn't sure what other child she thought he'd be asking about.

"Of course," she said with a tremulous smile. "The Tylenol kicked in, so his temperature is down."

"I didn't even know we had a thermometer."

"I found a new one still in its packaging in the medicine chest," Meg explained, then grimaced. "Unfortunately it's one of those old under-the-tongue ones."

"At least it works," Cole murmured, not about to let on that he hadn't known there was any other kind. "Okay, so the fever is better. How is he feeling?"

"Well, his throat is still sore but he fell asleep easily. And…no more vomiting."

Cole grinned. "Stellar news."

"Made me happy." Meg put a finger to her lips. "I think I'll sleep in the other twin bed in his room tonight. I want to make sure I hear him if he needs anything."

Cole thought of his mother. Her blood had flowed through his veins, but she'd always acted as if it was a huge imposition if he'd so much as asked for a sip of water when he was ill.

Charlie is lucky to have Meg for a mother. The thought was as reassuring as it was disturbing.

"I can get up with him tonight," Cole said. After all, sooner or later, there would be times when he would be the only one available to meet Charlie's needs. He couldn't afford to get too comfortable having Meg around.

"I already called the night shift," Meg said with a teasing smile. "How about you take care of him tomorrow when I'm craving a nap?"

Cole nodded, ignoring the relief rushing through his veins. "You've got yourself a deal."

"Now that that's settled…" Meg took a seat on the other end of the sofa. A sound of contentment slipped past her lips as she sank into the soft cushions. "I have to tell you, I am so ready to relax."

Her eyes lingered on the cup of steaming cider he'd

placed on the coffee table for her. "You sure know your way to my heart."

"You deserve it," he said.

Cole smiled when she immediately lifted the mug and took a sip.

Slipping one leg beneath her, she settled back on the sofa. "We both deserve it."

"True. But you're the one who took charge of Charlie this evening." Although Cole had wanted to care for his son, he knew she was best suited for the job. While his leg was much improved, getting a sick little boy into the shower and washing him up would have been difficult.

"I actually had the easy part," Meg said, sounding surprisingly sincere. "You had—" she grimaced "—to clean up the kitchen."

"You're right," he said with a decisive nod. "I deserve an extra cinnamon stick for taking on that lovely task."

Her laughter washed over him, as refreshing as a soothing tonic. Cole sank back into the leather cushions and decided if he ignored the fact Charlie had gotten sick, it had been a good day.

If Charlie was going to become ill anywhere, Cole was glad it had happened when the boy was surrounded by doctors and nurses Cole trusted. Having Travis check him out and David verify the symptoms matched a virus that was making its rounds in the area had reassured Cole it wasn't anything too serious.

Now his son was in bed and hopefully would get a good night's sleep and feel a whole lot better in the morning.

Which meant Cole and Meg had time to unwind. The cider tasted as good as it smelled. The crackling fire took any chill from the air. And, even in running pants and a T-shirt, Cole was comfortable.

"What kind of music is that?" Meg propped one stocking-clad foot up on the rustic coffee table.

"New age stuff." Cole waved a hand. "I thought about putting in a different CD but the melody is growing on me."

She cocked her head and listened for a few seconds. "You're right. Reminds me of a Gregorian chants CD I own, except with instruments. Definitely soothing and restful."

Cole had a feeling it wasn't simply the music from the lute Meg was reacting to, but the golden glow from the lamplight which complemented the warmth of the fire. The potpourri she'd brought home last week from the store also added to the ambience.

He'd teased her when she'd filled festive Christmas bowls and told him she was going to scatter them throughout the house. Now, the scent of peppermint mixed with cinnamon filled the air. Somehow, his house had begun to feel an awful lot like a home.

"I'm sorry we had to leave the party so abruptly," Meg said, taking another sip of cider. "You didn't even get to sample any of that scrumptious food Lexi made."

"I have to admit I had my eye on the poached salmon." Cole raised his cup to his lips but didn't take a drink. "Other than that, I didn't mind leaving. I've never been much for parties."

Meg chortled. "Don't give me that. In high school you had a reputation for being quite a party animal."

Cole tightened his fingers around the mug's handle. "Let's just say I never missed an opportunity to go where food was being served."

"Food?" Meg's eyebrow lifted. "What did that have to do with anything?"

It had everything to do with it, Cole thought. In fact, tonight, seeing the bountiful buffet table had brought back memories of those lean years. But they were in the past. No longer did it hurt to recall them.

"Are you sure it wasn't the liquid refreshments that drew you to those high school parties?" Meg asked with a teasing smile. "C'mon, you can tell me."

"I rarely drank back then." Cole shrugged. "I couldn't afford to get caught and kicked off the team. Plus seeing how booze ruled my stepfather's life made me determined to not go down that same road."

"Well, I never got invited to the parties, so drinking wasn't an issue for me." Meg laughed. "I think Travis made up for me. From what I heard, he did a good job representing the family at those kind of events."

Cole simply smiled.

"Are you hungry?" she asked abruptly. "There's some leftover chicken salad in the fridge. I could make us a sandwich."

While Charlie hadn't appeared impressed by the tarragon chicken salad Meg had made yesterday—asking for PB&J instead—Cole had thought it was terrific.

"Sure. But I can—" He started to push himself up from the sofa, but Meg waved him back down.

"Let me," she said. "It'll only take a sec."

Before he had a chance to protest she was already on her way to the kitchen. It seemed like she'd barely left when she returned with a sandwich for each of them and some fruit. Cole realized he must be hungrier than he'd initially thought, because the chicken salad on nine-grain bread and the cut-up apple slices with fruit dip looked like a feast.

"Wow," he said, taking the plate she handed him. "Very nice. Thanks."

"Anyone ever tell you that you're easy to please?"

Cole thought for a second then shook his head. "Only you."

He was still chewing when Meg placed her sandwich back on her plate.

"Why did you go to parties for the food?" she asked. "That doesn't make sense to me."

Cole slowly swallowed and didn't immediately respond.

"This is probably me worrying about nothing, but when I was getting the food together, I realized you'd made a statement and I just glossed over it. I think I do that a lot."

Two bright spots of color dotted her cheeks.

Cole knew he could make up something that answered her question but told her nothing. Or he could tell her the truth.

"Food matters," Cole said, "if you don't have enough to eat."

"Not enough to eat?" Meg pulled her brows together. She'd asked a simple question and he'd given her a riddle. "Why wouldn't you have had enough to eat? Your stepdad had a job."

Meg knew that for a fact. She'd seen Wally stocking shelves at the big-box store out on the highway with her own two eyes. She and Cole had been seeing each other at the time and she'd recognized the grizzled mountain-of-a-man as his stepfather. Instead of speaking, she'd walked on by and acted as if she didn't know him.

Now, looking back, she realized that had been rude. Of course, if she was ever granted a "do-over" on her teenage years there would be a lot of things she'd do differently. Knowing the man he'd become, Meg was sure Cole felt the same way.

"You're right. Wally did have a job. When he decided to show up, that is." Cole's eyes were dark and unreadable in the dim light. "But any money he earned went for booze and cigarettes and gambling, in that order. Having food in the house for two kids who weren't even his wasn't a necessity for him."

"Oh, Cole. I'm so sorry. I—"

"Don't." He reached over and took her hand. "I didn't tell you about my past to garner sympathy, only so you would understand."

His hand was warm and testosterone wafted off him in waves. Meg could have sat there all night, holding his hand, looking into his eyes, but all too soon he pulled his fingers away and sat back.

"I'd like us to get to know each other better." He dipped an apple slice into the fruit dip but didn't immediately bring it to his mouth. "To do that we have to be honest."

Meg experienced a jolt of déjà vu. Hadn't they already had this discussion? Yes, she was positive they had. "You're right. The better things are between us, the better it will be for Charlie."

Cole placed the uneaten apple slice back on his plate and turned slightly to face her. "It's not Charlie I'm thinking of…."

The air turned heavy with longing and Meg found herself drowning in the blue of his eyes. She reached out her hand and his warm fingers closed around hers again. This time she had the feeling he wasn't going to let go. Which suited her just fine.

"Cole," Meg began, not sure what she meant to say. But it didn't matter because one of the two cell phones on the coffee table chose that moment to go off.

She heaved a resigned sigh and met Cole's gaze.

"Is that yours?" she asked. "Or mine?"

A sheepish look crossed his face. "I'm not sure."

It hadn't taken them long to realize that not only did they possess the same smart phone—great minds obviously think alike and all that—but each phone had been programmed with the same basic ringtone. While he'd promised to change his, his response told her that task was still on his "to-do" list.

Regardless, the jarring ring had shattered the moment. Cole glanced at the display screen then handed the phone to her. "Your phone. Your brother."

She took the cell from his hands and shot him an apologetic look. "It's Zac. I really need to take this."

"Of course," he said. "Do you want some privacy?"

"Not at all. Stay right where you are." She clicked on the call. After several seconds of "can you hear me now?" the connection finally improved.

"It didn't even sound like you," Zac said. "I thought at first I'd reached some guy."

"Well, my voice may be a bit low but no one has mistaken me for a man before," Meg said with a smile. "Happy almost-Christmas, Zac. How are things with you?"

"I've been better." For the first time, Meg picked up on the strain in her brother's voice.

"What's wrong, honey?" she asked, falling back into that "mother" role with him. She had no idea whether he would share what was troubling him or skirt around the issue, but at least she had to try.

Growing up, Zac had been a closed book. It had been very difficult for her to "read" him. Yet, for the strain to be audible, whatever was going on must be serious. Out of the corner of her eye, she saw Cole look up from the newspaper he'd picked up and was pretending to read.

"I'm with Elisabeth's family for Christmas," he said. "That's what's wrong."

A shower of static drowned out the rest of his words. "Zac. I can't hear you. Call me back on the landline."

Meg quickly rattled off Cole's home number before the call was lost.

Cole lifted a brow. "Bad connection?"

Meg blew out a frustrated breath. "What else is new?"

She wondered if Zac would call back. It wouldn't surprise her if he didn't, but seconds later, the cordless phone rang.

"Sorry 'bout that," Meg said in lieu of a greeting when she picked up the handset.

"No need to apologize to me. I used to live in Jackson Hole," Zac reminded her in that brash manner she always associated with him. "I know all about the crappy cell reception in the mountains."

"Okay," Meg said with a laugh. "Apology retracted. Now, who's Elisabeth? And what are you doing spending the holidays with her family?"

"Elisabeth—Lissa—is my girlfriend," Zac said. "We've been together for a while now."

"It must be serious." As far as Meg remembered, this was the first time Zac had ever given her the name of a girl he was dating.

"I love her and she loves me," Zac said in a matter-of-fact tone. "We have a baby. His name is Henry. He's two months old."

"Henry was the child you were thinking of leaving when we last talked." Meg immediately regretted the comment. A wise woman knew to always gather her thoughts before blurting out something she might—make that, *did*—regret.

"I don't know where you got that idea. I'd never leave my son." An edge of steel ran through Zac's tone. "Never."

This time Meg took a second to consider her response.

"Of course you wouldn't," she said in a soothing tone, ignoring Cole's curious glance. "You and Lissa must be serious if you have a baby and are spending Christmas with her family."

For everyone's sake, she hoped it *was* serious. Though Meg was a thoroughly modern woman, she still believed little Henry would do best with both his mother *and* his father in his life.

"Lissa is an only child," Zac informed her. "She couldn't bear the thought of us not seeing her mom and dad at Christmas."

"Her being close to her parents is a good thing," Meg said slowly, gingerly finding her way. Those years of raising teenagers had schooled her in the dangers of making suppositions.

"It might be if they thought I was the right man for her," he said in a flat tone. "But they don't."

Meg fought against a motherly surge of indignation. Any family would be lucky to have her brother in it.

"Then they must not know you well enough," Meg said in a conciliatory tone, sincerely hoping that was their only reservation. "Because if they did know you, they'd love you like I do."

"Love." Zac gave a little laugh. "Right now I'd settle for *like*."

"Zac," Margaret began but stopped when she heard her brother talking to someone in the background.

"Margaret," he said after a couple of seconds, "I need to run. Have yourself a Merry Christmas with your new family. You deserve some happiness of your own."

"Wait, Zac, don't go. When are you going to call again?" Meg asked quickly before he could hang up. "I'd love to figure out a time when I can see you, meet Lissa and hold my new nephew."

"Soon," Zac said, then the line went dead.

Meg held the phone for several seconds before clicking off, trying to assimilate what she'd just heard.

"Everything okay?" Cole asked.

"My brother has a girlfriend and a baby, a little boy." Meg still found herself unable to wrap her mind around the thought that Zac was a father. "The baby's name is Henry, same as our dad."

Her lips curved upward. For a man who seemed to prefer the less traditional route in life, Zac naming his first-born after their father spoke volumes.

"Does Travis know?"

"I have no idea who Zac has told." Meg rubbed a hand across her face. She didn't want to talk about her brother. Not now anyway. She tilted her head. "What were we talking about before he called?"

"How much I enjoy being with you."

"Yeah, right."

"How beautiful you are." Cole leaned forward, catching up pieces of her hair, rubbing the shiny auburn strands between his thumb and forefinger. "How incredibly sexy…"

Meg's breath caught in her throat and her heart fluttered. This man definitely knew how to change a subject.

"There wasn't one woman at that party as gorgeous as you," he said in a deep husky voice.

Staring into the liquid blue of his eyes Meg almost believed him. Despite knowing that she could be over her head in seconds, there was something that drew her to him, that tempted her to take a step off the firm shore of what she'd always known and take a chance.

Before she knew what was happening, his mouth brushed hers, as soft as butterfly wings and just as gentle. Her lips were still tingling when he sat back. But if he thought he could get by with a drive-by kiss, he didn't know her as well as he thought he did.

Meg scooted close and wound her arms around his neck. "Lexi's house had mistletoe everywhere. When we were leaving I found myself thinking that it was a shame." She pulled her lips together to form a pout. "No kisses for Meg beneath the mistletoe this year."

Perhaps she should have stopped there. But she was having too much fun. She placed the back of her hand against her forehead and heaved a melodramatic sigh. "Poor, poor Meg."

She expected Cole to laugh. To her surprise, his expression turned solemn. "Are you telling me you'd have kissed me at the party, in front of all those people?"

"Well, I wouldn't have gone crazy and stuck my tongue in your mouth, if that's what's worrying you," Meg said with a throaty chuckle. "But you bet your cup of cider I'd have kissed you underneath the mistletoe."

A pleased look filled his eyes and his hand slid up her neck, getting tangled in her hair. "If you had kissed me, I'd have kissed you back. Just. Like. This."

Meg didn't have time to react when suddenly his lips were on hers. A firm kiss that let her know it wasn't going to end anytime soon. A surge of desire rose inside her. Her breasts tingled and an ache took up residence low in her belly.

As they continued to kiss, the weight of his body pushed her down onto the cushions. Moving from her mouth, his lips traced the line of her jaw, his breath warm against her throat. She shivered and arched her neck, reveling in the fiery sensations sweeping like an out-of-control wildfire through her body.

Meg wanted Cole in a way she couldn't ever remember wanting anyone before.

His hand closed over her breast just as a plaintive voice filtered down the stairs.

"Mommy. Daddy," Charlie called. "My tummy hurts."

Cole's hand stilled.

Meg's eyes met his. Her lips quirked upward. "Busted."

He grinned. "Again."

With a sigh of regret Meg pulled to her feet.

"Is he calling for Joy and Ty?" Cole pushed himself upright. "Or for us?"

"Does it matter?"

"Good point."

"I'm coming, sweetie," she called out loudly enough to reach the top of the stairs.

To her surprise Cold struggled to his feet. "I'm coming with you."

"But the stairs…"

"Don't worry. I won't slow you down," he said. "I'll follow."

"But—"

"I want to be there," Cole said. "I want Charlie to know that while you're there for him, I am, too. We're a family, after all."

Family. Meg sure liked the sound of that word.

Contentment slid through her veins like warm honey. She crooked her arm through Cole's. "On one condition."

"What's that?"

"If Charlie wants me to sing him to sleep like he did before, you have to promise not to laugh."

Chapter Fourteen

Two days later, even before Cole stepped out of the shower, he knew in his gut that it would be a good day. During the night the snow had stopped falling, the sun now shone brightly and his relationship with Meg was on the upswing.

When Cole saw the DNA testing kit in his underwear drawer, he experienced a surge of excitement. Ever since he'd arrived in Jackson Hole, he'd been waiting for just the right opportunity to get a sample from Charlie.

The little boy was used to the old-fashioned thermometer popping in and out of his mouth. Taking four cheek swabs should be a breeze. All Cole had to do was figure out how to get the samples in the mail.

With below-freezing wind chills, leaving a package out for the mail carrier didn't seem prudent. He could hardly ask Meg to hand it to the postman without prompting a slew of questions. And, at this point, he didn't want to in-volve her in this matter until he knew if Charlie was indeed his son.

After pulling on his jeans, Cole tugged a University of Texas sweatshirt over his head then put on his shoes. He secured the brace on his knee then opened the drawer again, letting his gaze linger on the package containing the testing supplies.

Yes, today *would* be a perfect day. All he had to do was figure out how to get the envelope in the mail.

"This is fabulous coffee." Meg peered at Cole over the rim of her mug. As far as she was concerned, nothing beat a good cup of joe in the morning.

"Umakkamecrazy is the perfect blend for any time of day," Cole said, sounding more like the CEO of the fastest-growing coffee chain in the United States than her housemate. "How was your night?"

Her lips tipped in a wry smile. "You mean after I ran into you skulking around the kitchen and screamed bloody murder?"

"Hey, I was thirsty," he said. "I was as surprised as you were."

Meg sincerely doubted that. At 2:00 a.m., she'd slipped downstairs to get a snack. When she'd bumped into a strong, muscular chest in the dark, she'd almost peed her pants. Nope, she could guarantee *she* was the one who'd been more surprised.

"It was a rough night," Meg said. "Charlie's stomach had him in the bathroom every couple of hours. Thankfully it seems better this morning and he's able to sleep. He didn't even wake up the last time I took his temp."

"You have to be exhausted," Cole said.

"I'm okay." Meg covered a yawn with her hand.

"Remember our deal." Cole slathered a thick swath of

grape jam across his toast. "I watch Charlie this afternoon while you take a nap."

"I haven't forgotten," Meg said with a sigh. "I'm just not sure there will be time."

"Why not?" Cole's gaze lifted from the toast. "We don't have any plans."

"We *didn't* have any plans." Meg stirred a spoonful of brown sugar into her oatmeal. "While you were in the shower, I got bombarded with phone calls. Our social calendar is now full."

Okay, *bombarded* may have been a bit strong for two calls. But considering the phone rarely rang, it had felt like a whole lot more.

"Who called?"

"Ryan." Meg glanced at her cell phone lying on the table and checked the time. "In fact, he should be here in about fifteen minutes."

"What's the occasion?" Cole asked, sounding only mildly interested.

"He didn't say." Meg had tried to pin down the smooth-talking attorney, but he'd been as slippery as Charlie at bathtime. "But I have a hunch he wants to talk to you about Kate."

Cole started to laugh then stopped when she didn't join in. "You're serious."

"While I don't know for certain," she said, "that was the vibe he was giving off."

"I hate to burst your bubble," Cole said, "but guys aren't like women. Ryan isn't going to spend all that time driving out here to talk about his girlfriend problems."

"Believe what you want." Meg took a bite of toast. "I grew up with brothers."

"I still say there has to be another reason for his visit," Cole said.

"I've given you my theory." Meg pushed back her chair, other worries on her mind. "I'm going to hop into the shower."

A thoughtful look blanketed Cole's face. "Before Ryan gets here I think I'll sit with Charlie for a few minutes. That way, if he wakes up, he won't be alone."

"That's nice of you, but not necessary," Meg said. "Last I checked he was sleeping very soundly."

"I'd still like to spend the time with him," Cole said.

"Well, if you need me I'll be making myself present-able for company." A tiny smile lifted the corners of Meg's mouth. "Just in case I'm wrong and Ryan does want to visit with me while he's here."

"You want me to do *what?*" Ryan's voice rose before the attorney reined it in and dropped it to a more conver-sational level.

"For God's sake, Ry, I'm not asking you to rob a bank." Cole spoke freely, not concerned about being overheard. Meg was upstairs while he and Ryan were in the first-floor office with the door shut. "Just drop off the envelope at the post office in town. It already has the correct postage, so you don't need to do anything else."

"Does Margaret know?" Ryan asked.

"Know what?" Cole shifted in his seat, hoping his impulsive decision to ask Ryan to drop off the envelope containing his and Charlie's DNA samples hadn't been a mistake.

When Meg had mentioned Ryan's visit, Cole realized the attorney could be his way of getting the samples in the mail.

"Does Margaret know you're doing a DNA test on the boy?"

Cole hesitated, not sure whether to confirm or deny

Ryan's suspicions. "You got all that from one envelope being sent to a lab?"

"Actually, the fact that Charlie looks like you was my first clue." Ryan leaned back in the tall wingback chair, his eyes devoid of the laughter usually found lurking in the gray depths. "Joy wanting to add you to the will, even though she'd already listed Margaret, was the second. I may not be smart enough to figure out a way to keep Kate from preferring Joel over me, but I'm not stupid."

Meg had been right, Cole suddenly realized. Ryan *had* come over to talk about Kate. He forced his thoughts back to the matter at hand. "All I'm asking is that you drop the envelope off on your way home."

"You are aware that by doing the test in this manner, the results won't hold up in court." Ryan's expression turned serious and Cole could almost see him putting on his lawyer's hat. "The chain-of-custody requirement won't be met."

"I understand," Cole said. "If this comes out the way I think it will, then I'll look at taking that next step."

"You like Margaret," Ryan said.

"Of course I do," Cole admitted.

"Then, as your friend, I suggest you don't keep this from her." Ryan dropped the envelope into his briefcase, snapped it shut and stood.

"It's not as simple as you're making it sound." Cole jumped to his feet and began to pace. "No matter what explanation I give, Meg will see the fact that Joy slept with me as a betrayal. I don't want her feelings for the woman she considered to be her best friend tarnished unnecessarily. Especially since I may not be Charlie's father. Joy told me herself that Ty was his dad."

"But you could have been," Ryan guessed.

Cole nodded. "The dates match."

"You do have yourself a mess." Ryan clapped Cole on his back and turned toward the door. "Tell Margaret and Charlie I said hello."

"Don't you want to stay? Talk about you and Kate? I assume that's why you dropped by."

Ryan surprised Cole by placing a hand on his shoulder. "I have to thank you."

"Thank me?" Cole cocked his head. "For what?"

Ryan grinned. "Your issues make mine look insignificant."

Ryan had barely walked out the front door when Meg waltzed down the stairs, dressed in jeans and a navy-and-white ski sweater.

"Was I right? Did he come to talk about Kate?" Meg asked.

Cole blinked. "What?"

"Ryan. Was his visit about Kate?" Her hazel eyes appeared green in the light. "Or something else? He looked pretty serious when he left."

"You were right. He came to talk about Kate."

"I hope you gave him some good advice," Meg said, her expression earnest. "After all, that's what friends are for."

She really was a good gal, Cole thought. So caring. So compassionate. The more he got to know this grown-up Meg, the harder it was to reconcile her with the girl who'd betrayed his confidence back in high school. "Ryan assured me he felt better about the situation by the time he left."

"I knew you'd come through for him." A warmth ran through Meg's veins. She was beginning to realize Cole was a guy you could count on. "I only hope things go as well with Ed."

"Ed?" Cole looked up.

"Ed Rice," Meg explained. "From high school. Tall.

Thin. Prominent Adam's apple. Some of the mean kids called him 'beanpole.'"

The muscle in Cole's jaw jumped. "I remember him."

"Well, apparently Ed is now the reading specialist for the Teton County Schools." Meg ignored Cole's less-than-enthusiastic reaction. "He asked if he could stop over and talk to us about Charlie."

"I didn't know you were still in contact with him."

There was an odd look in Cole's eyes. If Meg didn't know better she'd think he was jealous.

"Until today, I hadn't seen or spoken with him in years." Meg kept her tone matter-of-fact. "After our phone conversation, I'm now fully up-to-date. He married Brenda Carl. She was in the class behind us. They have two little girls and are expecting a baby boy in March."

"Good for him," Cole muttered. "Tell me again why he's coming over?"

Clearly something was bothering Cole. Tension was rolling off him in waves.

"So what do you think?" Meg kept her tone deliberately light. "Lunch before or after Ed?"

"I'm not hungry—"

"Lunch afterward, it is."

"You didn't answer my question," Cole said, trying but not quite pulling off a smile. "Why is he coming over?"

"I'm not sure." Unease settled across Meg's shoulders as she reviewed the conversation in her mind. "Come into the kitchen with me. I'll make some hot tea and tell you all about the conversation. It was very strange."

Cole followed her into the kitchen and took a seat at the table. "Strange how?"

Meg put the teakettle on the stove before sitting down opposite him. "I called Charlie's school this morning to let them know he was sick and ask if there was any homework I needed to pick up."

"Homework? He's only in first grade."

"Things have changed a lot since we were that age." Meg smiled. Back when she was Charlie's age they were just beginning to read. "Anyway, they put me on hold for the longest time, then Ed suddenly came on the line. For some reason the office staff at Charlie's school had patched me through to the district office."

"And?"

"Well, when I discovered it was Ed, I wasn't sure what to think."

"I remember you two being close friends."

Meg felt her cheeks warm. "Ed had a crush on me back in high school. I didn't return his feelings. It was… awkward."

Cole didn't look like he believed her but he didn't comment.

"What do you think he wants?" he asked instead.

"All he'd say is that he needed to talk to you and me about Charlie."

"He mentioned me?"

"He did." Meg didn't understand Cole's surprise. After all, Ed had Charlie's file. "I tried to find out more, but he just kept telling me not to worry, that we'd talk about Charlie when he came out."

Without warning, Cole reached over and covered her hand with his. "But you *are* worried."

Meg nodded, feeling the sting of tears against the back of her lids. She blinked them away, feeling foolish.

"I'm worried, too."

She looked up and for the first time saw the concern in his eyes.

"Whatever is going on with Charlie, we can handle it," he said. "He'll be okay."

"Because he has us."

"That's right." Cole got up to tend to the whistling teakettle. "We're in his back pocket."

Chapter Fifteen

Ed Rice took a sip of coffee. Though his demeanor was calm, Cole sensed he was nowhere near as composed as he appeared. For one thing, his Adam's apple kept bobbing up and down, and there appeared to be a sheen of perspiration on the top of his balding head. And he seemed to be avoiding Cole's gaze.

Perhaps Meg's suggestion that they meet in the kitchen had thrown the educator off his stride. He was dressed for business in a navy suit and red tie, and they'd placed him in a kitchen? Not to mention when they'd taken seats at the table, Meg had scooted her chair closer to Cole, as if wanting to make it clear where her allegiance lay.

At that moment, the tightness gripping Cole's chest had begun to ease.

"I was sorry to hear about Joy." Ed kept his pale blue eyes focused on Meg. "I remember how close you two were in high school. Rarely saw one of you without the other."

"Joy was special." Meg sighed. "I don't know that there was anyone I trusted more."

"*Both* Joy and Ty were special," Cole said.

For the first time, Ed shifted his gaze to Cole. "I forgot. You knew them, too."

"Joy was my neighbor growing up," Cole explained. "And Ty became a good friend later."

"Of course," Ed said. "That's how you ended up with partial custody."

"Meg and I have joint custody," Cole clarified. "We both love Charlie and are concerned about the reason for your visit today."

"While it's wonderful to see you again, Ed," Meg said, "I, we, really would like to know why you're here."

Ed cast a surreptitious look in Cole's direction, and suddenly Cole knew why Ed had come. The temperature in the room dropped thirty degrees in a heartbeat.

Please, God, no.

"Last year Charlie's teacher noted that he wasn't reaching the milestones that are set for children of that age." Ed spoke slowly, obviously choosing his words carefully. "He spoke with Ty and Joy, offering the opportunity for Charlie to participate in a program that would give him extra reading assistance."

"How's that been going?" Meg asked.

Time seemed to stretch and extend. Ed shifted uncomfortably in his wooden chair. "They declined to participate."

"What?" Cole straightened in his seat. "Why?"

"Parents opt out of the additional assistance for a variety of reasons," Ed said diplomatically. "They have to agree to work with the child every night for thirty minutes. Some won't—can't—commit to that amount of time."

Cole frowned. "That doesn't sound like Joy or Ty."

"I assume you're here because Charlie is still struggling." Meg's face held lines of strain, her tone as tightly strung as a piano wire.

"Charlie is still experiencing issues with his sounds and with letter identification," Ed said. "He's fallen even further behind where we would expect him to be reading. His classroom teacher reports he's been acting out during reading time."

Meg glanced at Cole then back at Ed. "Because of his parents' deaths?"

Ed shook his head. "It's been going on since the beginning of the year."

"He's doing it to divert attention from his difficulty reading," Cole murmured.

After the tiniest hesitation, Ed nodded. "That would be my guess."

Cole took a deep breath and asked the question burning a hole in his brain. "Do you think Charlie could be dyslexic?"

"Dyslexia is a possibility." Ed cleared his throat. "His school's reading specialist happened to be in the classroom one day observing the children and noticed Charlie was writing his letters backward."

"Doesn't dyslexia run in families?" Meg looked perplexed. "I know Joy wasn't dyslexic. I don't think Ty was, either."

"It's frequently found in families." Ed tapped his Montblanc pen against the tabletop. "Where dyslexia is identified, up to half of these children have a history of learning difficulties in their family and more than half have a family member who is left-handed."

The color faded from Meg's cheeks. "Charlie is left-handed."

"So is Cole," Ed observed, his Adam's apple bouncing up and down like a jumping bean.

"We're here to talk about Charlie." Cole's jaw tightened with annoyance. "What are your recommendations?"

Ed opened his briefcase and pulled out a thick packet of papers. "I brought with me the participation packet for our reading assistance program as well as some suggestions for some multisensory games you could play with the boy over the holiday break. If you want to sign the agreement now, I can take it back with me and we can get him started when school resumes in January."

Cole made no move to pick up the packet lying where Ed had placed it on the table. "Thank you for bringing these out. Meg and I will discuss this and get back to you with our decision."

Ed's lips thinned. He'd obviously expected them to sign on the dotted line. While Cole had little doubt that they would have Charlie participate in the program, this was something he and Meg needed to discuss first.

"I can't stress strongly enough the need for early intervention." Ed fixed his gaze on Cole. "You should know better than most the challenges children face when they get older and can't read well."

"Yes." Cole gave a bark of laughter that lacked humor. "I've experienced how cruel kids can be."

Ed flushed. He glanced down at his papers for a long moment then lifted his gaze. "I've owed you an apology for a long time. This is probably as good a time as any to say I'm sorry. I look back on what I said to you and, well, I can't believe I was such—"

"A jerk," Cole filled in the blank.

Meg's gaze shifted from Cole to Ed, a frown furrowing her brow. "What did you say to him?"

The blotches on Ed's neck, just above his shirt collar,

deepened to a ruddy red. "Some remark about him reading at a fifth-grade level."

"You knew Cole was dyslexic?" Meg's surprise appeared genuine. If Cole didn't know better he'd have been convinced. "How did you find out?"

Cole cast a sideways glance her way. "You told him."

"Me?" Meg's voice trembled with outrage. "I most certainly did not."

"That's what he told me." Cole may have spoken to Meg but his gaze remained focused on Ed.

Meg's eyes flashed green fire. If looks could kill, Ed would already be dead. "Ed?"

The man went very still for a moment. "I was your father's student assistant that semester. I overheard you asking your dad for ways to help someone who couldn't read well."

Ed blew out a breath before turning toward Cole. "Meg refused to give him a name, but I knew you were seeing each other and I put two and two together."

"How did you know I was seeing him?" Meg asked.

"I—I had this crush on you," Ed said. "I was aware of everything you did."

Cole listened to Meg chew Ed out with only half an ear, stunned by the realization that he'd blamed her all these years for something she hadn't done.

The thought of how wrong he'd been was still running through his head when they walked Ed to the door, promising to get back to him with a decision after the first of the year.

Cole pushed the heavy front door shut behind him, then turned to face Meg. "I thought it was you who'd told Ed my secret."

"That's why you dumped me." Her eyes widened as she

made the connection. "You believed I'd broken your confidence."

"Ed told me the two of you had laughed about me being so stupid. He said that's why you didn't want anyone to know that we were dating."

"That man is lucky he isn't standing in front of me right now," Meg sputtered. "I'd never have done something so despicable. Never."

"I know that now." Cole moved from the foyer to the window in the great room, feeling restless, his thoughts as tangled as the swirling snow.

Cole fought against the cold invading his body, the aloneness invading his soul. Then Meg wrapped her arms around his waist from behind and rested her head against his back.

"I wish you'd have come to me," she whispered in a low tone. "Given me a chance to explain, instead of believing the worst."

He heard the pain in her voice and the disappointment.

"I was seventeen. Even if you'd explained, I don't know that I'd have believed you." Cole turned to face her, reassured when she kept her arms around him. "You were brilliant."

Meg gave a strangled laugh. "Hardly."

"You were to me." He traced the gentle curve of her jaw with one finger. "And so beautiful."

Cole stared at her for a long moment. "I couldn't believe anyone like you could love someone like me. Ed's comments just solidified that belief in my head."

"Oh, Cole." Tears filled Meg's eyes and she wrapped her arms around his neck. "I'm so sorry. So very, very sorry."

"I'm sorry, too," he said. "I wish I'd handled things differently. I made a decision about your character based on my teenage-boy insecurities."

"It's okay." She expelled a shaky breath. "We've been given a second chance. That's more than most people get."

Cole realized with a sense of amazement that it was true. She could hold his distrust against him but she didn't. Meg was a beautiful woman, inside and out.

"We'll be more open and honest with each other this time. We'll listen and share and there'll be no more secrets." Meg gave a tearful laugh. "We know how destructive those can be. No, this time we'll be starting over with a clean slate."

This was his opportunity, his chance to tell her about Joy and him. Would she forgive him? And more importantly, would she forgive Joy?

Women were funny about their friends. Even today, Meg had alluded to how much her friendship with Joy had meant. No, there was no point in bringing up that Joy had slept with him. Not until he knew for certain that Charlie was his son.

"I can't believe we're snowed in on Christmas Eve." Meg turned back from the window. For as far as she'd been able to see, a thick blanket of white covered the ground.

"It's Jackson Hole in the winter." Cole looked up from the whiteboard where Charlie was writing simple three-letter "sight" words in different-colored markers, and held up one hand. "Good job, cowboy. Punch it."

Meg shifted her gaze just in time to see Charlie bump Cole's fist with a force that would have done a boxer proud.

"I did it, Aunt Meg." Charlie flashed a brilliant smile and pointed to the whiteboard. "That says 'dog.'"

"Yes, it does." Meg's heart swelled in her chest until it felt as if it would burst. She wasn't sure who she was most proud of—Cole or Charlie.

When Cole had told Ed they'd get back to him about

the reading assistance program, she'd feared that like Ty and Joy he would opt out of the extra assistance. Perhaps he didn't want Charlie labeled. Perhaps he didn't want to commit to the time and effort in the evenings. After all, she knew how much time he'd been spending on the phone with his corporate staff.

Then, after Ed left, she'd asked Cole about it. No more of this wondering or speculating. Honesty was now at the heart of their relationship.

Meg had almost started crying when he'd said this was an important decision they needed to make together. It was then she knew that they'd truly turned a corner in their relationship.

Charlie glanced up, a bright blue marker in his hand. "How is Santa going to find our house with all the snow?"

The day after Lexi's party, she and Cole had planned to take Charlie over to her brother's house in the afternoon so they could shop for "Santa" gifts. Charlie's illness had derailed those plans.

"Good question, Charlie," Cole said. "I have no doubt Santa will eventually make an appearance, but I doubt it will be tonight."

Charlie's face scrunched up and tears filled his eyes. "There won't be any presents?"

"Just because Santa is delayed doesn't mean the three of us can't give each other gifts," Meg said. "When I was a little girl, my brothers and sisters and I used to make presents for each other in addition to getting gifts from Santa."

"What did you make these gifts out of?" Cole asked.

Charlie cocked his head, tears clinging to his long lashes, listening for her reply.

"Just items we had around the house." Meg forced enthusiasm into her voice.

"That sounds like a lot of fun," Cole echoed, jumping in to help her sell the idea to the little boy.

"What would you make?" Charlie asked, still skeptical.

"We'd draw pictures or make paper dolls or—"

"Paper dolls?" The look of disgust on the boy's face made Meg smile.

"You and Uncle Cole may not want to make dolls for each other," Meg said, trying not to smile, "but you could make one for me. There are all sorts of things we can make."

"I'm in," Cole said. "How 'bout you, Charlie?"

The little boy thought for a moment then nodded. "Okay. But I don't want no doll."

Chapter Sixteen

That night, after presents had been exchanged and Cole had finished reading *The Night Before Christmas* in front of the fire, he and Meg found themselves alone on the sofa. His arm rested comfortably around her shoulders and a Kenny G Christmas CD played softly in the background.

The ficus tree had been decorated with red and green chains made out of construction paper, interspersed with handmade ropes of popcorn and cranberries.

The gifts they'd opened earlier in the evening lay on the coffee table before them.

"We probably should have taken Charlie's presents up to his room," Cole said. "He's not going to be happy when he wakes up in the morning and discovers he left them behind."

"I'll bring them up with me when I go to bed." Meg's gaze dropped to the picture book Cole had made him. It sat next to the stuffed sock dog Meg had sewn, complete with button eyes and a yarn tail.

"When he saw the dog," Cole said, "he was as excited as if you'd given him a real puppy."

"I think it would be good for him to have a dog," Meg said.

"I agree."

"You do?"

Cole nodded. "Ever since you did that get-acquainted exercise the first night we were together and we discovered we're all dog lovers, I've been thinking a puppy would be good for Charlie."

Meg hesitated. "There'd be some logistical stuff we'd need to figure out. Like would the puppy stay at one of our places all the time or would it go back and forth with Charlie between your house and mine?"

"I was thinking it'd be nice if the puppy and Charlie only had one home to go to." Cole's eyes looked black in the dim light.

Meg's heart skipped a beat. Was he saying what she thought he was saying?

But she didn't have a chance to ask, because all of a sudden his lips were on hers and nothing else mattered except her and him and the closeness.

When Meg left his bed at two o'clock Christmas morning, Cole realized how much she'd become a part of his life. She'd brought a richness, a fullness to his existence that he hadn't even known he'd been missing.

He didn't want her in his life on a temporary basis, he wanted her there permanently. Filling his nights and days with warmth and joy. Being a mother to Charlie and a wife to him.

I love her.

The realization came as no surprise. From the moment he'd seen Margaret Mary Fisher in that crowded school hallway, he'd known she was the one for him. And regardless of what the DNA tests might show, Charlie was his son. No, *their* son.

Cole thought of the papers his attorney had prepared, the ones which would petition the courts for sole custody once paternity was established. He thought of the fact that Meg still had no idea that he and Joy had once had a brief relationship.

He'd initially decided not to tell her about his involvement with Joy if the paternity test came back negative. Now he knew that he had to tell her regardless.

Meg valued honesty and so did he. She'd been right when she said they'd been given a second chance. A chance he didn't want to blow.

Hopefully the roads would open up and he could slip into town to do some quick shopping. Though he could tell she liked the glitter heart he'd made her, he had a more special gift in mind.

A gift that would show her how much he cared.

A gift that would pave the way for a declaration of love…and an overdue confession.

Three days after Christmas, the holiday spirit still filled Meg's heart. She let her gaze linger on the glittery silver heart on the black construction paper before shifting to the necklace made out of macaroni shells. Both now sat on her dresser. A lump formed in her throat.

She couldn't imagine ever receiving two nicer Christmas gifts. Carefully picking them up in one hand, she moved them to the bed then resumed dusting. When she was done, she returned them to what she liked to refer to as their "place of honor."

Having them next to where she placed her earrings guaranteed they were the last things she looked at before she went to bed…and the first things she saw every morning.

Just seeing them made her smile and brought back that warm Christmas glow. That's why she'd made it clear to Cole that she didn't want another gift. But he didn't appear to be taking her seriously. She suspected that's why, when Ryan had stopped over, he'd jumped at the chance to ride back into Jackson with him. Unless he really was going "stir-crazy" like he'd said.

Or he might just want to pick up more supplies to use in working with Charlie.

Meg pressed her lips together, her heart hardening at the thought of Ed and his lies. All she could hope was that experience would be a lesson to her and Cole to always keep the lines of communication open.

She quickly finished her dusting then returned to the living room, where Charlie had Lincoln Logs scattered from one side of the large room to the other. But instead of happily playing with them as he'd been only minutes before, he lay on the sofa, fast asleep.

Meg crossed the room and covered him with a cotton throw, brushing a kiss on his cheek. "I love you, Charlie."

Love.

Even though it had been less than a month, Meg realized she'd fallen in love with the little boy…and with his new daddy.

Of course, she had a sneaking hunch she'd never quite fallen *out* of love with Cole Lassiter.

"I love you, Cole," she murmured to herself, the words feeling right and true on her tongue.

Did he return that love? If her intuition was on target, he did. The look in his eyes when his gaze settled on her, the gentleness and passion in his touch all spoke to deep feelings.

When she'd mentioned last night in passing that the only open jobs for a physical therapist in Jackson Hole were part-time, he'd encouraged her to apply, saying those hours would work perfectly. Between the two of them they could be there before and after school for Charlie.

While she didn't want to presume too much, he knew as well as she did how expensive rent was in Jackson Hole. She could never afford to do it on a part-time salary... unless she continued to live with him.

The yearning that rose inside her both scared and thrilled her. Thrilled her because she couldn't imagine being anywhere but by his side. And scared her because she loved him and had been hurt by him before.

Still, her worries were buoyed by the knowledge that she now knew the truth about what had happened all those years ago. All the secrets were out and there should be nothing preventing them from moving on.

Meg had just finished putting the last Lincoln Log into its canister when she heard a familiar ringtone coming from the kitchen.

Although she knew she was being foolish, fear sent her heart into overdrive. By the time she scooped up the phone, she was out of breath as if she'd run a long race instead of simply gone from one room into another.

When Cole had left this morning, she'd resisted the urge to tell him not to go. The roads were snow-packed and icy. Meg knew how treacherous these mountain roads could be....

"Hello," she said, her heart pounding in her ears.

Static filled the air for several seconds before she heard a man's voice.

"Cole, this is Brian. We've got a lousy connection. Can you hear me?"

"Yes," Meg said. "But this isn't—"

"I received the results of the DNA testing on you and Charlie this morning," Brian continued. "I thought you'd want to know right away."

DNA testing? What was the man talking about?

"It's as you suspected all along. Charlie is your son, so that is indeed good news." Brian's tone, which had been friendly, suddenly became more businesslike. "I have the papers ready to file for sole custody. I'll email those for you to sign along with the papers from the lab."

More static filled the line.

"I'll be back in touch soon," Brian said before the line went dead.

Meg stood completely still for the longest time, her—er—Cole's phone in her hand, processing what she'd just heard.

Cole was Charlie's father, not Ty. How could that be? Joy and Ty had been a couple for almost ten years.

Had Cole donated his sperm to help Joy conceive? But if that were the case, wouldn't Cole have already known he was Charlie's biological father? And why would both Cole and Joy have kept that fact a secret from her?

Unless...

No. Meg shoved from her mind the image of Joy and Cole with naked limbs entwined.

There had to be a logical explanation for all this. She couldn't wait for Cole to get home so she could find out what it was....

His good day had taken a nosedive. Cole realized something was wrong the second Meg met him at the door and he saw the look in her eyes. At first he worried that something had happened to Charlie, until the little boy burst around the corner and tackled him.

"Everything okay?" he asked in a low tone over the top of Charlie's head.

In response she cast a pointed glance at Charlie. "We'll talk later."

Cole didn't want to wait. But it appeared he didn't have a choice, not with Charlie happily chattering about all the things he'd done while Cole had been in town, and tugging on his hand, asking him to play Lincoln Logs with him.

He placed the sack of learning supplies for Charlie on the side table in the foyer, keeping the smaller sack with him.

"I need to drop something off in my room," he said to Charlie, "then we'll play."

Meg pulled a phone from her pocket. "You might as well take this with you. It's yours."

"Sorry 'bout that." Cole grabbed an identical one from his coat pocket and handed it to her. "I didn't realize I'd taken yours until Ryan and I were already in Jackson."

She didn't smile or make a joke about him stealing her phone. Instead, as they exchanged phones, her gaze kept shifting from him to Charlie.

If Cole didn't know better, he'd think she suspected… Nah, that was simply his overactive imagination mixed with a large dose of guilt.

Still, as he headed to his bedroom, his sixth sense told him something was wrong and it involved him and Charlie. Surely his attorney wouldn't have sent something to the house. Cole had made it very clear to Brian that any communication regarding Charlie's paternity was to be by email or phone only.

Phone.

Cole stepped inside his bedroom and pulled the door

shut. Only then did he pull out his phone, the one Meg had returned to him only moments before. He went immediately to the recent calls. When he saw Brian Danaher's name at the top of the list, Cole's heart stopped.

Taking several deep, steadying breaths, he hit Redial.

"Brian," he said immediately when the attorney answered. "It's Cole."

"I bet you've been doing some celebrating today."

"Celebrating?"

"About the positive DNA test results." Brian paused. "How much of what I told you did you hear?"

"Remind me what you said." Cole dropped down to sit on the bed. "I want to make sure I heard it all."

"Well, to summarize—you are the boy's father. I've emailed the paper to petition for sole custody," Brian said. "Like we spoke about before, we'll need to do another DNA test following the strict chain-of-custody protocol for it to hold up in a court of law."

"About those papers," Cole said. "I'm going to hold on to those for now."

"You said earlier that you wanted to move quickly on the custody issue." Brian's tone was filled with puzzlement. "Is something wrong?"

A sick feeling filled the pit of Cole's stomach. "I really hope not."

Chapter Seventeen

The next five hours were the longest ones of Cole's life. He was hypersensitive to every look, every comment.

Like at dinner when Meg said, "I noticed before that you and Charlie are both left-handed."

Charlie didn't make things any better when he proudly announced that his hair stuck up in the back just like his uncle Cole's.

Though Cole had planned to have a very different conversation with Meg this evening, while he picked at his food over dinner, he tried to convince himself that it was good they were having this conversation now. Now that it had been confirmed Charlie was his son...

Shifting his gaze from the log cabin he was building on the floor, Cole settled it on the little boy, overcome with love for this child of his.

When he finally looked up, he found Meg staring. Her

expression gave nothing away, but the flash of pain in her eyes before her lids dropped told the story.

He prayed he could make her understand. If not, he feared that the life he wanted—the one that had been within reach only this morning—would be gone.

When Charlie's bedtime rolled around, the three of them took turns reading from an age-appropriate storybook. Tonight it was Charlie's favorite, the one about farm animals.

Cole had informed her that a dyslexic child's reading could be improved if they read aloud. Apparently it had something to do with activating the "Broca's area" in the child's brain, which remembers speech muscle movement.

But instead of admiration over his desire to help the boy, all Meg felt toward Cole was disgust. How could he have lied to her? How could he have made her believe that he wanted them to be a family when all along he planned to cut her out of Charlie's life? Based on what his attorney had said, plans were already in place that would kick her to the curb.

Well, she wasn't unwanted baggage, she was a vital part of this little boy's life.

Charlie caught her staring and smiled. She gave him a thumbs-up. "That was really good, sweetie."

Meg dropped her hands to her side and clenched her hands into tight fists. If Cole thought she'd just walk away from this boy she loved, well, he'd find out soon enough what happened when you shook a mother lion's cage.

"Aunt Meg." Charlie's sweet voice broke through the churning in her brain. "It's your chance to read."

"You almost missed your turn," Cole joked.

Meg met his gaze, the smile on her lips only for Charlie's benefit. "You'll find it's not that easy to cut me out."

Cole didn't say a word, but she knew he'd gotten her

not-so-subtle message. An observation that was confirmed once they'd put Charlie to bed.

He took a seat on the sofa and gestured for her to sit beside him.

Meg reluctantly dropped into a nearby chair.

"It's not my intent to cut you out of Charlie's life," he said, his eyes dark and serious in the lamplight.

"Yeah, right."

"I'm telling you the truth."

"Who are you?" Meg's voice sounded shrill, but she didn't care. *Truth.* Did he even know what the word meant? "I feel like I never knew you. Not back in high school. Certainly not now."

"Look, I'm sorry you had to find out Charlie is my son this way." Cole raked a hand through his hair. There was so much he wanted—make that *needed*—to say to her. But when he'd planned this discussion in his head, it hadn't been with her glaring at him.

"Yes, that did come as quite a surprise." She gave a humorless laugh. "I just wonder why it took me so long to see it. It's obvious now when I see the two of you together."

"Meg, I didn't—"

"When were you planning to kick me out, Cole? Your leg is almost healed. Were you waiting for the doctor to release you before you told me I'm out of his life? Or were you going to just let me get the legal papers in the mail?"

Cole had initially assumed it'd be best to let Meg talk. Give her the opportunity to blow off some steam. He realized that had been a mistake. She reminded him of a locomotive being stoked by misconceptions. A head of steam was building and any moment she could blow.

"You know, I'm getting this déjà vu feeling all over again," she continued before he could respond. "Following your own agenda is what you do best. You pretend to have feelings for me then you drop me. You haven't changed at all."

"Meg," Cole said. "Please let me explain."

"Explain?" She practically sneered the word. "Or make up a few more lies?"

"Yes, explain." Cole spoke between clenched teeth.

She crossed her arms and lifted her chin. "Okay. You can start by *explaining* to me how it happened that you and my best friend had a baby together."

Despite her adversarial tone, Cole told himself this was progress. At least she wanted—okay, was willing—to hear what he had to say.

"Joy and Ty were going through a rough time in their relationship." Cole chose his words carefully. "She wanted to get married and Ty wasn't sure he did."

"So you muddied the waters by sleeping with her."

Cole ignored the comment and continued. "She left Jackson Hole and moved to Texas. I'm not sure why she chose Austin other than her great-aunt Mary lived there. Joy and I ran into each other and started hanging out. Both of us were lonely and one thing led to another. We only had sex a couple of times before we realized you shouldn't sleep with someone when you're in love with someone else."

"Wow, what a revelation," Meg drawled, sarcasm dripping from each word.

"Joy loved Ty. It wasn't long before he realized the mistake he'd made in letting her go and came to get her. They married in Las Vegas on their way back to Jackson Hole."

"Then Joy found out she was pregnant." The hurt in Meg's eyes tore at his heart. "And both of you let Ty think it was his."

"I didn't find out she'd even had a baby until her aunt

mentioned it when she stopped by the coffee shop one day. By that time, Charlie was already eight months old."

"Really? She didn't call or say anything to you about it before then?"

Her tone called him a liar.

"That's right." Cole held on to his temper with both hands. "As soon as I heard about the baby I came to Jackson Hole. When I asked, Joy insisted he was Ty's baby, not mine."

Cole would never forget that day. Anger. Hurt. Sadness. He'd experienced a whole cacophony of emotions in one short hour. "When I mentioned doing a DNA test, Joy began to cry. She told me I would ruin her marriage if I pursued the test. And it would be all for nothing because the test would show Charlie was Ty's son."

"You didn't believe her."

"I didn't know what to believe."

"You walked away from your own son."

"She insisted he wasn't mine." Cole wiped a hand across his face.

"I can see how she could have fallen under your spell and lived to regret it," Meg said, her words a sharp knife to his heart. "I did."

"Everything," Cole said with a fierceness that surprised both of them, "*everything* I said to you I meant."

Meg rose and moved to the window, her back now to him. "You meant it when you said you wanted the three of us to be a family."

Cole stood. "Every word."

"Yet you told your attorney to get the papers ready to file for sole custody." Meg turned and reached inside the neckline of her cowl-necked sweater. She pulled out the silver heart he'd given her their first—and only—

Valentine's Day together. "I put the necklace on this morning because I saw us having a bright future together."

Cole's heart dropped when she flung it on the table and shook her head, a look of disgust on her face.

"Meg, listen," Cole began. "Let me explain."

"You listen. You will *never* take Charlie from me." An edge of steel ran through her tone. "I'll never walk out on that little boy and my promise to his mother."

"This is not as horrible or as unworkable as it appears." Cole forced a conciliatory tone. "Let's sit down and talk this through."

"I don't trust you and I don't want to be with you anymore." Meg met his gaze. "As soon as I find a place to live, I'm moving out and I'm taking Charlie with me. There's nothing you can say—or do—that will change my mind."

Cole had just gotten off a conference call with his attorney, finalizing plans for the Jackson Hole franchise, when the home phone rang again.

He snatched it up, cradling the receiver lightly against his ear. "Don't you have anything else to do on New Year's Eve but talk with me?"

"May I speak with Margaret, please?" a man's voice said. "Tell her it's Zac."

Meg's youngest brother. Hearing the affection in her tone for this man, Cole had once looked forward to meeting him.

"Zac, this is Cole Lassiter. Your sister isn't here. She's out running errands."

It was true to an extent and it sounded a helluva lot better than saying she was checking out several apartments that had made her short list.

"I tried her cell," Zac said, his frustration evident. "The call kept dropping before it went through."

Cole grimaced. Cell reception was a sore subject with him, too. "The weather is bad here. Must be affecting the signals again."

Zac swore. "Do you know when she'll be back?"

"No clue." Cole told himself to stay out of it. He might be Meg's family, but whatever problem he had was none of Cole's business.

Her brother blew out a harsh breath.

Not my concern, Cole told himself. Still, he knew how much Meg loved Zac. And Cole *could* drive into Jackson and track her down…if the situation was critical.

"Is there something I can do?" Cole asked. "Does this have anything to do with your girlfriend and baby? Are they okay?"

"Yes. No. I don't know."

Silence filled the line for several long seconds. Cole waited, not about to press.

"Margaret told you about Lissa and the baby."

"She did," Cole said. "Congratulations."

"Lissa and I, well, we're not together anymore."

Cole waited for him to elaborate, but all he heard from the other end of the line was the sound of a bottle top popping open.

"What happened?" Cole clamped his mouth shut, but the question had already slipped past his lips.

"Her old man got his way." Zac's tone was heavy. "Her parents think I'm not good enough for their princess."

"What do you think?" For some reason, Cole couldn't seem to pay attention to the "none of my business" refrain in his head.

"I may not have a college degree but I do okay," Zac said. "Ian is an engineer and he doesn't come close to what I earn most years."

Cole clicked on the gas log and heat began to flood the

room. Something told him this might take a while. "What is it you do?"

"Custom welding. Ornate gates, fences, decorative doors. Stuff people pay big money for," Zac said. "Lissa's dad is a three-piece-suit kind of guy. That's the kind of man he wants for her."

Cole knew how much that had to hurt. Even though back in high school he'd been irritated that Meg hadn't told her parents they were seeing each other, his irritation had been tinged with relief. What would Mr. and Mrs. Fisher have thought of him? He doubted they'd have approved of a C-student who lived with a stepfather cops knew by name for all the wrong reasons.

"What does Lissa think?" Cole asked.

"She's proud of me," Zac said. "She wants to marry me. Or at least she did...."

After a long moment, Zac continued, "She told me I was using her dad as an excuse. That I was scared to commit. Can you believe it?"

"Is it true?"

"Hell, no," Zac retorted. "One thing is true. Her old man isn't going to rest until he drives me totally out of her life."

"Seems to me whether you stay together is up to you and her, not to him."

"Yeah, well, whatever." From Zac's tone, Cole knew the conversation was over.

"I'll tell Meg you called."

"Were you really going to take the kid from my sister?"

Cole inhaled sharply. Of all the things Meg believed, that hurt the most.

"Is that what she told you?"

"Answer the question, Lassiter."

"I considered it...at first. But that was a mistake in judgment. Meg is Charlie's mother now. He loves her and she loves him."

"What about you?" Zac asked. "Do you love Margaret?"

Cole fought the urge to sweep the love he felt for Meg under the rug like he'd done for so many years. But to say he didn't love her would be a lie. And he was done lying, to himself and to others. "I do."

"Did you tell her you didn't plan to take the kid from her?"

"She doesn't believe me," Cole said. "I tried to explain that I wasn't going to file the papers, but she wouldn't listen."

"Make her listen."

"She's already made up her mind. You can't change a woman's mind."

"The hell you can't."

Cole smiled even as he recalled how he'd begged and pleaded with his mother not to go. His stepfather had laughed, telling him he was wasting his breath. A woman makes up her mind to leave, and that's that....

Of course, Wally was hardly an authority on relationships. For the first time in days Cole felt a glimmer of hope. He would try again. And again. And again. As many times as it took for her to forgive him and believe he was sincere.

"Margaret is worth the effort," Zac said, as if he could somehow read his thoughts from hundreds of miles away. "Whether you choose to try is up to you."

Cole paused. "You know, I believe you just gave me the same advice I gave you."

Zac laughed and the line went dead.

Chapter Eighteen

New Year's Eve Day

Meg sensed something was different the second she walked through the front door. Perhaps it was because Charlie wasn't running up to greet her. While she'd been out looking at apartments, Travis had called and asked if he could pick up Charlie and have him spend the night.

Saying that the twins would be easier to handle if they had a friend to play with didn't make sense to her, but she didn't argue. Meg knew Charlie would enjoy himself. And since Cole had mentioned something about going to a party with Ryan tonight, she'd have the house to herself.

Though it meant she'd be ringing in the New Year alone, at least she wouldn't have to walk on eggshells all night. Having to be around Cole these past couple of days and pretend everything was okay for Charlie's benefit had been difficult. But soon, she promised herself, soon she'd have a place of her own. She wondered why the thought didn't make her happier.

"You're home."

Meg's head jerked up from the packages she was juggling in her hands. Cole stood in the kitchen wearing jeans and a denim shirt that brought out the blue in his eyes.

"I thought you were going with Ryan tonight."

"Change of plans."

"Kate unexpectedly available?"

"Something like that." He gestured with one hand toward the oven. "I have pizza."

"I'm not hungry—" To Meg's horror, her stomach chose that exact moment to complain about her skipping lunch.

"It's hand-tossed pepperoni from Perfect Pizza."

Meg could feel herself waver. Her favorite kind from her favorite place. Of course, she could always have the leftover meatloaf in the fridge. "Okay. One slice."

It was the adult thing to do, she told herself. And she and Cole needed to try to get along—at least superficially—for Charlie's sake.

He held out his hand.

She drew back. Surely he didn't expect her to put her hand in his? No matter how good he smelled or how handsome he looked, that wasn't happening.

"Your coat." The twitch in his lips told her he'd read her mind. "I'll hang it up while you put your bags away."

She could feel the heat rise up her neck. If she'd been thinking clearly she'd have known that's what he wanted. One thing she had to say for Cole, he'd always had the nicest manners. "Thank you."

As she handed the coat over to him, their fingers brushed. A flash of heat traveled up her arm. She wondered if he felt it, too. But she didn't look at him, because it didn't matter.

Still, seeing him, being near him, brought those old feelings flooding back. Perhaps having dinner together wasn't such a good idea, after all.

"You know," she said slowly, "I'm really not that hungry."

Instead of joking around and trying to keep things light as he had the past couple of days, his expression grew serious. "This could be one of our last evenings together. It'd be good to get some closure, to not leave anything that we want to say to each other unsaid."

A feeling of pure panic rose inside her. Meg didn't want to talk anymore, to think anymore, to hurt anymore. "I've already said everything."

"You don't have to talk. Have a slice of pepperoni and just relax."

Meg hesitated. It wouldn't take long to eat one slice. And, she reminded herself, he *had* followed through and promised in writing not to pursue sole custody. Not to mention he hadn't tried to push her out the door. If he could make a few big concessions, she could make a small one.

"Okay. I'll put these sacks away and meet you in the kitchen." Meg walked away without waiting for a response, wishing she had the guts to simply ignore his request.

When she reached her bedroom, she dropped the sacks on the bed. But instead of hurrying down the stairs, she took a moment to run a brush through her hair and put on a little lipstick. Not for Cole, she told herself, but because looking her best would give her the confidence she needed to get through one slice of pizza.

He smiled when she walked into the kitchen. The table was set with a red-and-white-checkered cloth, topped by a bouquet of daisies.

She widened her eyes when she saw the centerpiece,

unable to stop the rush of pleasure. "Daisies are my favorite flowers."

"I remember."

Meg wasn't sure what to make of the comment, so she turned her attention back to the table. For some reason Cole had chosen to use Fiesta plates instead of the paper ones they usually brought out when they had pizza. A can of her favorite cola sat next to a glass of ice on the table.

But it was the photograph next to Cole's plate that drew Meg's attention. She gestured with one hand toward the snapshot. "What is that?"

"I found it when I was going through my stuff. I thought you might like to have it." He pulled out her chair and stood behind it, waiting for her to take a seat.

The tantalizing scent of pepperoni hung in the air, and Meg knew that even if she wanted to walk away, her stomach—and curiosity—wouldn't let her. She only hoped they could eat in silence like they had the past couple of days.

Once Cole was settled in his seat, with pizza on his plate and soda in his glass, Meg picked up her slice. She took a bite, the pepperoni spicy against her tongue.

She looked up to find Cole's gaze on her, his eyes dark and inscrutable. Her heart skipped a beat at the raw emotion simmering in his eyes.

A sudden ache of longing for what might have been washed over her, startling her with its intensity. Meg found herself blinking back unexpected tears.

If Cole noticed, he gave no indication. After she'd returned the napkin to her lap, he slid the picture across the table until it rested in front of her.

Meg glanced down. She couldn't help but smile. She vividly remembered when the photo was taken. For February 14, the day had been surprisingly warm. She and Cole had taken a walk in the Elk Refuge after school. That's when he'd given her the silver heart necklace. Not long after that, he'd asked a stranger to take their picture.

Cole had a huge smile on his face, his arm looped around her shoulders. Her cheeks and lips looked rosy in the photo but the color hadn't come from the cold. Before the older couple had caught up to them on the path, she'd given Cole a "thank you" kiss and he'd reciprocated by giving her an even more passionate one back.

"It was a perfect day," he said into the silence.

"It was." Meg turned her attention back to the pizza. But the stabbing pain in her chest made swallowing difficult.

"I was happy when I was with you," Cole said in a quiet voice, his eyes taking on a faraway look. "Though looking back I realize that the whole time we were dating I was afraid."

Afraid? Back then Cole had seemed larger than life to her. Not afraid of anyone or anything. "Of what?"

"I knew if your folks found out we were together, they'd convince you I wasn't good enough for you." He shrugged and took a bite of pizza. "They'd have been right."

Was he joking? The serious set to his jaw said otherwise. Still, what he'd said made no sense. "How could you ever think that?"

"Well, for starters, my family life was one big mess and I was barely passing my classes." Cole's chuckle held no humor. "You have to admit, my future did not look bright."

"You were a good guy. Hardworking. Kind. You always stood up for the underdog."

Meg stopped. Was she actually defending Cole's character?

"I didn't feel good about myself back then. In school I was such a failure...." He stopped and a look of resolve filled his eyes. "I swear I will do everything in my power to make sure Charlie grows up feeling strong and confident, both in and out of the classroom. Every time I think of Joy and Ty turning down the reading assistance for him, it makes me angry."

"I don't understand that, either." Meg shook her head. "All I can think is maybe it wasn't explained clearly to them. But then I don't understand Joy telling you Charlie wasn't your son, either."

Meg realized she'd put all the blame on Cole the other night. But she had to admit that Joy had behaved badly and put him in a very difficult position.

"I like to believe that people make the best decision they can at a given time," Cole said. "Joy was under a lot of stress. She loved Ty and didn't want to lose him."

His generosity of spirit could have surprised her, but it didn't. Cole Lassiter really was a good guy. Her infallible intuition had told her that fifteen years ago, but she'd let hurt and anger guide her actions. Oh, if she only knew then what she knew now....

"I think a lot of people look back on their lives and wish they could have a do-over." Meg sighed. "I've wished that many times myself."

"A do-over?" The look on his face would have been funny at any other time.

"You know, a chance to go back and do something again, but this time do it right, with all the knowledge and maturity you didn't have at the time you made your initial decision." Meg thought of Joy and Ty and how much they'd loved their son. "If Joy and Ty were given a second chance, I like to think they'd make different choices. But they don't have that opportunity."

The thought made Meg sad.

"We have that chance, Meg," Cole said, his voice filled with passion. "This is our opportunity."

Meg pulled her brows together. "I thought we already discussed the matter and decided that Charlie should be in the program?"

"I'm not talking about Charlie," Cole said. "I'm talking about us."

Her heart fluttered wildly in her neck. "What are you saying?"

"That if I had a chance to do it over again, I'd have gone immediately to you after I'd spoken with Ed all those years ago. I'd have given you a chance to explain, like you're giving me a chance to explain now."

Here he was again, taking on the burden for that time when, if she'd have kept her mouth shut, the outcome might have been totally different.

"I shouldn't have said anything to my father." When Meg had heard Ed's account, she realized that while it was true that she hadn't given Cole's name, his story hadn't been hers to tell. "I promised I wouldn't say anything to anyone about your reading difficulties. Even though I didn't give my dad your name, and I asked him for help only with the best of intentions, I broke that promise. I hope you can forgive me."

"I can," Cole said. "And I do."

Their gazes locked and a moment of understanding passed between them. Healing, cleansing in its intensity.

Meg took a sip of soda and realized she felt better. His absolution had lifted a burden from her shoulders she hadn't known she was carrying.

Cole cleared his throat. "If I had to do it over—" He paused as if reconsidering. "No, I can't honestly say that I'd never have become involved with Joy, because that would mean Charlie wouldn't be here."

"The thought of you two making love—" Meg gave a little shudder. "It's very difficult to accept."

"Joy and I had sex. You and I make love. Very different." Cole's tone gentled. "But Joy was right. It's wrong to have sex with one person when you're in love with someone else."

"Joy loved Ty."

"And I loved you." Cole studied her face then smiled. "Don't look so surprised. Joy came to realize that she loved Ty and I realized I'd never stopped loving you. I wouldn't be surprised if she set up the will so she could do a little otherworldly matchmaking."

"But she knew how much you'd hurt me." Meg fought the sting of betrayal. "I don't understand how she could have had a friendship with you, much less slept with you."

"Joy and I grew up together. We were both lonely. That's all I know." Cole reached over as if to take her hand but seemed to think twice and sat back. "I don't want to talk about her tonight. I want to talk about us."

Meg traced an imaginary figure eight on the tablecloth with her finger. "What more is there to say?"

"Well, for starters, I'm sorry I didn't tell you that Charlie might be my son," Cole said, and when Meg looked up she could see the sincerity in his eyes. "I am sorry, you know. Very sorry."

"You didn't tell me because you were planning to take him away from me," Meg said.

"That is something else we need to clear up." Cole took one of her hands in his, relieved when she didn't try to pull away. "I set up that plan with my attorney early on when I thought I couldn't trust you. But my feelings changed and I saw things more clearly. You are Charlie's mother now. I would never take him from you. I should have told Brian I'd changed my mind, but I was so excited about where our relationship was headed that—"

"Our relationship?"

Cole smiled. "Give me a second."

He left the table for a few minutes then returned with a small box wrapped in shiny silver paper with a fat white bow on top.

"Merry Christmas," Cole said, placing it in front of her.

"I can't accept—"

"Please," he said. "Just open it."

Meg picked up the box. She'd carefully removed the bow and set it off to the side, when a thought struck her. "Since we're clearing everything up tonight, I have a couple of questions for you."

He glanced at the still-wrapped gift. She could almost see him rein in his impatience. "Sure. Ask away."

"Did you by any chance have something to do with Travis calling me and asking Charlie to spend the night?"

Cole nodded. "It was my idea."

"And Zac?" Meg asked. "He called me today and asked me to tell you thank-you."

"Your brother and I talked the other day," Cole said. "But actually he helped me more than I helped him."

"Good guy," Meg murmured, recalling that's how Zac had described Cole.

"What did you say?"

"Nothing." Her curiosity satisfied, Meg returned her attention to the gift. She tore off the paper, lifted the lid and found a shiny silver heart, the size of a big paperweight, inside. "It's beautiful."

"Open it," Cole urged.

Meg lifted the top off the heart then cocked her head. "Shredded paper?"

"That's the petition for sole custody," Cole said. "A petition that will never be filed."

"Well, thank you for that," Meg said, feeling disappointed but not knowing why. Oh, heck, who was she kidding? She'd found herself hoping that she and Cole might get a real second chance. "The heart is lovely."

"That's not all," he said. "There's something in the paper."

Her pulse gave an excited leap. In seconds she'd found it. She couldn't keep from smiling. "It's a ring."

Cole rose to his feet then dropped down to one knee beside her, lifting the diamond gently from her trembling fingers. "There's one part of my life that I wouldn't want to change or 'do over,' and that is meeting and falling in love with you."

Meg simply stared, blinking rapidly.

Taking that as a good sign, Cole continued. "I love you, Margaret Fisher. I always have and I always will. You would make me the happiest man in the world if you would agree to be my friend, my lover, my wife…and Charlie's mother. Together we will forge a life based on honesty, mutual respect and, above all, love. Will you, Meg? Will you be my wife?"

Her lips began to tremble.

His stomach clenched.

Then she smiled, a brilliant smile that lit up the whole room and sent hope flooding through the deepest recesses of his heart.

"When I thought you were going to take Charlie from me, I vowed to fight for him because love is worth fighting for." She reached down and took the ring from his outstretched fingers, twisting the large emerald-cut solitaire so that it caught the light and sent bright sparks of color shooting through the room. "When we started speaking about do-overs, I realized that it wasn't just you who'd made mistakes. I'd made some doozies, too. But like you, my love for you is something I never want to undo."

Cole's heart pounded loudly in his ears. "Was that a yes?"

Meg slipped the ring on her hand then flung her arms around him, peppering his face, his jaw with kisses. "Yes. Yes. A thousand times yes."

All he'd ever wanted was reflected in her eyes. Love. Trust. And the promise of a lifetime of happiness.

Laughing with relief and sheer joy, Cole rose and pulled her tight against him, knowing that at last all was right in his world.

The rest of the night passed in a blur. When the New Year's fireworks sounded over Grand Targhee and Snow King, Cole and Meg barely noticed.

They were too busy celebrating their love by making their own kind of fireworks.

Epilogue

Valentine's Day

"I thought this was supposed to be a small, intimate wedding reception," Cole teased his bride as they danced together across the shiny hardwood floor of the Spring Gulch Country Club.

"When you have seven siblings and one of them has five children, it gets big in a hurry." Meg rested her head against Cole's black tux, reveling in the strength beneath the fabric and the steady beat of his heart. "I'm glad the country club had a cancellation and we could have the reception here rather than at the house."

She and Cole had wanted their wedding to take place on a date that was meaningful to them and not too far in the future.

Unfortunately they'd discovered that a lot of other engaged couples felt the same way about February 14. Every reception venue they checked out had been booked for over a year.

They'd resigned themselves to having a very small family-only affair at home, when the Spring Gulch Country Club events manager called and said they'd had a cancellation.

Friends and family had sprung into action and pulled together a beautiful wedding and reception in six short weeks.

Meg lifted her head from Cole's shoulder, still swaying in time to the music, the silver heart around her neck glittering in the light from the antler chandeliers.

"Look at Zac and Lissa," she said in a low tone. "Don't they look happy?"

"They do. Just like newlyweds are supposed to look." Cole's gaze settled on the couple dancing next to Zac. "I didn't realize Chip had a girlfriend."

"She works with him at the grocery store." Meg smiled. "Seems like love is in the air."

"I love you, Mrs. Lassiter."

"I love you, Mr. Lassiter."

Suddenly his lips were on hers and the world around them ceased to exist. Lost in the passion of his body pressed against hers, all she knew was that he was her friend, her lover and now her husband.

"See, he's kissing her again," Charlie said in a loud voice just as the band quit playing.

Out of the corner of her eye, Meg saw Charlie—looking adorable in his tux—pointing to her and Cole, her brother's two mischievous boys at his side.

"Just wait," Charlie added. "Pretty soon he'll be on top of her."

A twitter rolled through the crowd.

Meg buried her face against the lapel of her husband's tux.

Cole laughed aloud. "You're absolutely right, son. You're absolutely right."

* * * * *

A sneaky peek at next month...

Cherish™

ROMANCE TO MELT THE HEART EVERY TIME

My wish list for next month's titles...

In stores from 15th February 2013:

☐ Her Rocky Mountain Protector – Patricia Thayer

& The Soldier's Sweetheart – Soraya Lane

☐ Fortune's Unexpected Groom – Nancy Robards Thompson

& Fortune's Perfect Match – Allison Leigh

In stores from 1st March 2013:

☐ Resisting Mr. Tall, Dark & Texan – Christine Rimmer

& The Baby Wore a Badge – Marie Ferrarella

☐ Ballroom to Bride and Groom – Kate Hardy

& Cindy's Doctor Charming – Teresa Southwick

Available at WHSmith, Tesco, Asda, Eason, Amazon and Apple

Just can't wait?

0213/23

2 Free Books!

Get your free books now at
www.millsandboon.co.uk/freebookoffer

Or fill in the form below and post it back to us

THE MILLS & BOON® BOOK CLUB™—HERE'S HOW IT WORKS: Accepting your free books places you under no obligation to buy anything. You may keep the books and return the despatch note marked 'Cancel'. If we do not hear from you, about a month later we'll send you 5 brand-new stories from the Cherish™ series, including two 2-in-1 books priced at £5.49 each, and a single book priced at £3.49*. There is no extra charge for post and packaging. You may cancel at any time, otherwise we will send you 5 stories a month which you may purchase or return to us—the choice is yours. *Terms and prices subject to change without notice. Offer valid in UK only. Applicants must be 18 or over. Offer expires 31st July 2013. **For full terms and conditions, please go to www.millsandboon.co.uk/freebookoffer**

Mrs/Miss/Ms/Mr (please circle)
_____

First Name
_____

Surname
_____

Address
_____

_____

                                        Postcode
_____

E-mail
_____

Send this completed page to: Mills & Boon Book Club, Free Book Offer, FREEPOST NAT 10298, Richmond, Surrey, TW9 1BR

Find out more at
www.millsandboon.co.uk/freebookoffer

Visit us Online

0113/S3XEb